BLACK CHERRY

Editing by Susan Keillor and Victoria Wilder

Front Cover Image by Midjourney and L.M. Bennett

Illustrations by Olga Begak

Book Design by L.M Bennett

Compiled by L.M. Bennett

Printed in the United States of America

First Printing, February 2020

Second Printing, September 2023

ISBN: 978-0-578-63635-1

L.M. Bennett Books

11923 NE Sumner St STE 879421

Portland, Oregon 97250

lmbennett.com

In loving memory of Zae.

Contents

Self-Deflection

Dujuana Sharese

You are absolutely stunning.

You are the embodiment of beauty. You are the quenching of Isis flooding my existence. You are the misunderstood hot spring geysers that provide unpredictable heat. Your depth of concern is beyond Yarlung in Tibet. I want to lose myself in the slippery pockets of your rainforest.

I can barely contain myself, I am so attached to you. Come to me, as though I know you are not worthy of all I have. But I will give it to you anyway. Come close to me because if not you, then who? So let's do this.

I was presented with the gift of translation. I can decipher your intentions within five blinks of your eyelashes. I can read in between your lines, comprehend the hieroglyphics written in script, and decode the graffiti tattooed on your lips.

I see you.

I'd seen the outcome before you said hello. So why didn't I go? I will make you my world. Let's waste time together, as we fall not in love with each other. But we will act like we are. Please, come closer to me. We can grow accustomed to each other's company and bond over habitual infatuation. I will tell you all of my secrets for your entertainment, so you will have ice breakers for your next event. Come close to me because if not you, then who? Let's do this.

I stayed to participate in the annulations.

I know you are not good for me. I know what I need. I'm pretty bright and resourceful. So why must I bask in the torture of your after math? I am sensually engrossed with a mystery that touches deep within my psyche. I can see your mother's anger in your smile. I feel the torment radiate from the fifth layer of your skin. You're begging for a soothing from the tension you are in. We are like-minded; we both meet on a plain of false hope to avoid the truth.

It will hurt.

She surrounded my planet with her story, all was aligned. When she finished destroying what was left, my timid atmosphere defying laws of gravity, she then drifted away in an abyss to make her own universe with someone else. How do I survive after the asteroids have been launched?

Can my planet survive another senseless impact? Would I be left with so much damage that I could not gravitate towards the light? Would she leave behind global warming, forcing me to drink my way through snow caps to receive nourishment? Will the vegetation grow back? Will my weeping willows bend, their locks linking with soil for life to breathe? Or will the sun meditate in ruins, casting no glow until I find peace? I am left with a stale chill that can be seen with balmy breath. Will the moon perpetuate false prophets as the stars brighten shadows? Will sickness spread in my determinations? Will my ambition survive the tsunami of selflessness? Can I rebuild a vibrant society without judgment and fear? How shall I gather the pieces of matter I lost from too many explosions, from too many implosions?

Why didn't I go?

Why didn't I go?

Because she was my freedom.

My freedom from reality TV pharmaceuticals, soothing the self-hatred that burned cable boxes and boy scout mottos.

My freedom from communistic karma sutra and oppression from melanin deep-rooted in sin. I Live in my freedom from Fox along with CNN.

She was my freedom from fatherless children who frequently witness puppets in politics. We see Jane run, but we call Dick the President

Free from the magic acts and smoke and mirrors hidden beneath the bills they passed right in front of us.

She was my freedom from uncertainty and instability of social security.

She was my freedom from mothers sacrificing children to worship false Gods of Celebrity.

I needed the pain of freedom, for she was the only one who could free me from myself.

A Tanka for Assata

L'Monique King

Pretty butterfly
soaring above blossoming
trees that sway in spring,
you are the sky's confetti
fluttering on life's sweet breeze.

7/5/07 - 2/13/20

Dear Assata,

As Valentine's Day approaches you are on my mind and always in my heart.
I wonder where you are and what you're doing. It plagues me to not know if
you're happy or for that matter, what makes you sad. I ponder frequently...have

you thought of me any time recently and if you have, what might those thoughts be?

I pray you are coming into your own mind, know that love is for anyone who can share and receive it and that you're not preoccupied with any anti lesbian nonsense, because the love I have for you is real. Trust me when I tell you Butterfly, THIS ain't no phase. My need to live truthfully is as authentic as my love for you. Of this I am certain, for the idea of holding you in my arms causes them to ache from your absence. The thought of not hearing your voice drowns out any sound I might hear Feeling the warmth of the sun on my face is yet another reminder of the painful void your absence creates, as I imagine what your cheeks would feel like, nestled close to mine. Assata, you are the girl I've always wanted. The girl whose hair I've dreamt of playing in. The girl I want to eat butter pecan ice cream and fried pickles with. Not together, though they're both good, as I've discovered since moving to the south twelve years ago before you made your arrival in New York. My mother still talks about visiting you in the hospital and how beautiful you were as I continue to fondly gaze at and cling to the picture she took of you. Twelve years is a long time to be disconnected from someone. However, not a day goes by that I don't think of you. My Butterfly, filled with color, growing, changing, soaring.

As you may know, I do have a very special someone in my life—someone to share the day with. We're married, still in love and have been together twenty-three years now. She's more than a spouse, she's also my friend. Yet and still, this "Heart Day" I'm choosing to focus on you—directing all my energies out into the universe, asking that my wish of seeing you soon might be granted. You see, Valentine's Day isn't just for lovers. It's also for grandmothers who have never met their grandchild/ren. You, Dear Butterfly, are still my one and only—so, when you think of love, when you think of Valentine's Day, please think of me, Me-Ma, your grandmother—as I await the day when love overtakes intolerance and we finally have an opportunity to meet...maybe before you turn thirteen.

Eternally,

Me-Ma

Spanish Sky

Unique Lee

Señora,

I am all ablaze

like the BLUSH of your cheeks

when I whisper the sweet melody of a temperate breeze in your ear

like a tongue turned SIENNA

from delving into warm, wet spaces

leaving remnants of chills in its undertow

like the FUSCIA engorged fire

roaring within your thighs

where GOLD bubbles up

like the richest honey

leaving in its wake

the scent of LAVENDER on a summer's eve.

My love for you burns

with the fervor

of a thousand Latin sunsets.

Nina

Amor Jomei

"Nina, can we go? We've been in the mall for five hours and you've been to every store. If you haven't found an outfit by now, then you just aren't going to the New Year's party," I said with half irritation and half boredom.

"Whatever, Sky. You know I have to slay these girls when I step out," Nina replied, ignoring my desire to leave.

"Yea, yea, yea. Just hurry your ass up."

"Don't rush me. I have to make sure my thirst traps are set for the New Year. I'm manifesting a new zaddy in 2020," she said as she continued to look around the same section she's gone through three times in the past thirty minutes.

If she wasn't my best friend of over twenty years, I would have left her ass in the mall and not thought twice about it. However, she was, and here I sat with bags of clothing and shoes for what she said was for tonight. With all these bags, I'm not sure if she knew this was a party and not a weekend celebration.

I watched as she tried on outfit after outfit. Everything fit her perfectly, but she couldn't settle on one dress. I was beyond tired and ready to go. I got up and went looking around the store for something that she hadn't already tried on. Rack after rack I shuffled through until my eye caught this black and silver dress. It was simple but eye-catching.

"Here, try this one," I said as I practically shoved it in her hands.

"What is the—?"

"Just try the dress on Nina, dang," I say in total frustration.

"Okay, okay...Sheesh. Calm your ass down," she replies as she retreats to the dressing room.

A couple of minutes later, I hear my name.

"Sky, what do you think?"

I look up to find that dress wrapped around every curve she possessed, oh so snugly. She looked beautiful. My mouth was hanging on the floor.

"Well, are you going to say anything?" she asked, bringing me back to reality.

"Damn...You look astonishingly beautiful" I managed to say.

The way she looked in that dress took my breath away.

"So, you think I should get it?" she asked.

"Yes, that has your name written all over it," I replied.

"Alright, now I have to find some pumps and accessories then we can go," she said.

After seeing her in that dress, I didn't care what we did.

Nina Love. Funny her last name was Love because that's what I was. In love with her. I had been since we were in high school. Now here we were, thirty-six and thirty-four years old and still best friends, yet she didn't have a clue that I was craving her in the worst way.

She was the sexiest woman on Earth in my eyes. I'm not talking about the superficial model or video bunny sexy. No, she was the "homegrown, cute, girl-next-door, with a touch of city girl" type. She was 5'2", 135 lbs of curves, mocha-cinnamon complexion, mid-shoulder-length hair, with the most intoxicating brown eyes you've ever seen. When she looked at me, it sent chills through my body. I loved it. I loved her.

An hour later and we were finally on our way home to get ready for the night.

"I'll pick you up around 10:45 pm. Tell Dani and Ashton to meet us there at 11:15 pm. Kai said she'll be there waiting for us," I said as I dropped Nina off at her condo in Midtown. I turned on Gucci Mane's 'East Atlanta Santa' as I made my way to my loft in Lil 5 Points.

Two hours later, I'm dressed in my New Year's Eve outfit: a black velvet blazer, black turtleneck, black and gold pinstripe pants, with black a pair of badass Zara chelsea boots with the gold cuban link chains, complete with gold accessories of course. My locs were freshly retwisted and my pores oozing with Y by YSL. I check myself in the mirror again, grab my keys, leather jacket and head out the door to pick up Nina to get the night started.

"I'll be pulling up in five minutes. BE READY." The text I sent read as I got off the exit.

Ten minutes later...

"Hey babe, I'm outside," I say to her as I hear her answer her phone.

"Okay, I'll be down in a few," she responds.

Fifteen minutes later...

"What is this woman doing? I told her to be ready when I got here. She knows I hate waiting for her when we have somewhere to be," I say to myself as I sit in the car listening to Quad City DJ's "What You Want For Christmas.

"11:00 p.m" is what my watch reads.

"Man, I hope parking isn't ridiculous at the club. Hell, the line too. I know she better hurry up, though."

Just as those words left my lips, I looked up to see a little slice of heaven and hell. Nina had done it again...left me speechless. She was drop-dead gorgeous. She had put her hair in loose curls all over, that smoky effect on her eyes to make them pop, and had on some fierce silver 4-inch stilettos to match her dress. Yeah, that dress. The dress that hugged every curve on her body so damn right. I loved how it stopped mid-thigh, giving you an eyeful of those juicy thighs and the way it pushed her breasts up and together, giving her enough cleavage to make your granddad's dick hard.

I got out of the car to open the door for her, nearly tripping from staring so hard.

"You alright, Sky?" she asked as I caught myself from falling.

"Yeah, I just slipped on the gravel. That's all," I responded. "You look amazing, Nina. Like, seriously."

"Well, you know...What can I say?" she said, cockily. "Naw'll, seriously, thank you. I hope to meet someone tonight and I hope I don't run into Jess's crazy ass. I'm trying to bring in my new year with no drama and without her bi-polar energy."

"Don't worry, baby girl. Tonight will be one for the books. Believe that," I said as I drove off in the direction of the club.

"Ten seconds to 2020!" DJ Dimples said on the mic to all the party-goers.

"10...9...8...7...6...5...4...3...2...1!! Happy New Year!!" the crowd screamed.

Confetti and balloons fell from the ceiling and women all around hugged and kissed. I hugged Nina and kissed her on her forehead. "We made it, babe. I love you," I told her.

"I love you too," she responded.

I hugged and kissed the rest of the crew and told them I was going to find some more of my friends, and I'd be back. I partied and danced with my other homies for the next hour and headed to the restroom. As I stood at the sink washing my hands, I heard some commotion outside the restroom, and it sounded like Nina and Dani's voice. I dried my hands off and went to investigate. As I walked out the door, I see Dani standing between Nina and Jess.

"Just leave her alone, Jess. You're crazy and she doesn't want anything to do with you. You threatened her life and that was the last straw. Enough is enough," Dani screamed.

"Fuck that. She is going home with me tonight. I'm not leaving without her," Jess said as she reached to push Dani out of the way.

"Slow your roll, shawty," I said as I pushed Jess against the wall. "Nina isn't going anywhere with you as long as I am here. So, chill the fuck out and go find some other broad to put up with your shit. There's plenty here to choose from."

"Let me go. I don't give a fuck what you're saying. Nina's coming home with me tonight," she said as she struggled to get loose from my grip.

"I'm not going to argue with you, but you heard what I said, and I dare you to go against my word. I've been itching to whoop your ass. Nina felt sorry for your condition and told me not to, but I give two fucks about it and will lay you out right here if you even so much as look her way. And let that be my first promise of 2020," I said with venom in my voice. "So, I suggest you walk in the opposite direction when I let you go. Got that?"

"Yeah, man, whatever," she said through her teeth as I let her go.

We watched as she walked off into the thick of the crowded club.

"Y'all okay?" I asked the girls.

"Yeah, we're cool," they said.

"You sure you're okay?" I asked Nina.

"Yeah, she just kind of messed my mood up a little."

"Come on, let's go to the bar and get some drinks. If you want to leave, just let me know and we'll bounce," I tell her as we head to the bar.

Two hours later, and we are dead tired after having the time of our lives. The party was still jumping, but I noticed Nina's actions started to slow, indicating that it was about that time.

"You ready to go, Nina?" I ask her.

"I think I am. My feet are tired and I'm ready to take a long hot shower and get in my bed to relax. Are you ready? We can stay longer if you want to still hang."

"Naw'll, I'm good. We can bounce."

"Aight, cool. Let's tell the gang we are headed home then," she said.

We exchanged hugs and kisses to the crew and left the club.

"You want to stop at Waffle House to get something to eat?" I ask as I get off her exit.

"Naw'll, I'm not hungry. I'll just fix something if I get hungry later."

"Aight, cool," I say as we turn down her street.

"Ugh. I don't have time for this shit tonight," I hear Nina say, breaking me from my brief moment in space.

"What is it? What's wrong?" I ask with concern.

"That's Jess's car parked in my driveway. I can't deal with this. I refuse."

"Don't worry about it. You can crash at my house," I tell her as I drive past her condo and make a right onto the next street to circle back around to the entrance.

"I just don't understand why she won't leave me alone. I sat and listened to her cry, then yell and scream at me for two hours, and then she acted like nothing happened the next day. I told her whatever we had was over and I've been ignoring her calls and texts for three months now. Exactly how long does it take to sink in a person's head that it's over?" she rambled.

I listened to her vent the entire ride to my house. It angered me to see her so distraught over someone who was never worth her time in the first place. I felt like sometimes women took her kindness for weakness and ran with it until she was left with nothing more to give. I hated that. I hated to see her hurt over and over. I wanted to protect her from all these wannabe fuckbois, abusers, and psychopaths, but I had to let her live her life. I couldn't rescue her forever. She had to see people's true colors on her own. She had already been through a lot, but each day I see her growing stronger and stronger. I wanted to be her Superman, but I understood that she was becoming her own Superwoman.

We pulled up to my loft and prepared to get settled in the house.

"You know the drill. You know where everything is and can stay in your usual room. I'm about to fix me something to eat and make some tea. You sure you don't want anything to eat?" I ask.

"No, I'm fine. I don't have an appetite right now. I'm going to take a hot shower and relieve some of this tension. Thank you for everything tonight," she replied.

"It's no problem. I will always have your back. Let me know if you change your mind and want something to eat."

"Okay, I will," she said as she left the room looking tired and defeated.

I watched as she walked slowly into the room to shower. She was in her feelings and it hurt me so badly. I wish I could just erase all her pain away. She deserved to be treated like the queen she was. She deserved to receive what she gave others but each time she came up short and broken.

I got all the ingredients out to cook, but my mind and heart were focused on Nina. I wanted her. I had to tell her exactly how I felt about her. She deserved to know that she was my world. That I wanted nothing more than to love her wholly and unconditionally. I couldn't wait any longer. The thought of sitting back and watching her get hurt by some other selfish fool was beyond logical. Fuck it, I had to let her know. It was now or never.

I walked to the guest bedroom and headed straight for the bathroom. I opened the door to the bathroom and stopped in my tracks at the silhouette in front of me. Her shadow from the steam in the shower and dim lighting did something to stir the lustful beast inside me. I started to strip off my clothes as I watched the slow, rhythmic movements of Nina bathing herself. I pulled off the last sock and opened the shower door. She jumped.

"Sky, what are you doing—?" she started to ask.

"Shh...please don't speak," I whispered.

"But—" was the only thing she managed to get out before I kissed her.

Every emotion that I've ever felt for her came through in that kiss. I slowly made love to her mouth and entangling my tongue with hers. She wrapped her hands around my neck, releasing a low moan of pleasure and caressing my head as I pulled her closer. Electricity shot through me as our bodies touched. I wrapped my arms around her waist as my head swam from the passion growing between us. I had to break the kiss.

"I want you and you need me right now. Can I have you?" I whispered as I looked in her eyes.

She stared at me with her eyes filled with passion and shook her head yes.

At that moment, I began to kiss and lick the water off her neck, gently biting as I squeezed her breasts. She gasped and released a soft moan. I trailed my tongue down her neck. The further I ventured with my tongue, the further south my hands went. I placed kisses on her breasts, as I lightly brushed my fingers over her sweet valley.

I could already feel her pulsating beneath my fingers. That excited me. Flicking my tongue over her nipple, I took it in my mouth. A low moan escaped from deep within her. I slowly and gently began to suck on her nipple as only a newborn could. Back and forth, back and forth my fingers stroke her clit as her body responded and matched my rhythm. Gradually increasing my speed, I sucked harder on her nipple as I rolled the other between my fingers.

"Mmmm, Sky, baby. Please don't stop. Please," she said in between moans.

My response is slipping my fingers deep inside her love tunnel. She is so wet that I'm able to slip three fingers inside her hot, pulsating hole. Her juice gushes out with each stroke as she bucks her pelvis against my hand.

gasps "Sky!! MMMmmmm. Oh, baby. Deeper!" she screams.

I go deeper and massage her clit with my thumb. My sexual hunger is raging as I suck and pull her nipples with my teeth. Deeper and deeper, faster and faster, my fingers stroke.

"Oh shit, Sky. I'm going to cum! Yes, baby, yes!!" was all she managed to say as her body began to convulse. I dropped to my knees, lifted her leg and began licking her pussy. The contact of my tongue must have sent a wave of electricity through her body because she started to climax again. I tongue fucked her and swallowed every last drop of her sweet juice. I was in heaven, but far from causing hell on her body.

I picked her up and carried her to the guest bed. I'm glad I decided to keep the heat on when we left for the club because I didn't have time to dry her off. I immediately flipped her over on her stomach, pulled her up on her knees, and spread her ass cheeks. I licked her from the "roota to the toota" as us Southerners would say. I circled my tongue around her ass and caressed her clit with my fingers. She started to rock and moan to the rhythm. I made my tongue as hard as a rock and slowly fucked her ass and love tunnel.

"Shit, that feels so fucking good." She moaned as she threw her ass back on me.

"Yes, baby! Fuck my ass. Fuck my pussy!"

Harder and faster, I drove my tongue in her ass and delivered the same treatment to her tunnel.

"Fuck, Sky, I need you inside me! I need you to fill my insides with your dick, baby. Now, baby, now!" she screamed as she bucked wildly on my tongue.

Sweet music to my ears.

I practically ran to my room to get my strap. I swear it took me three seconds to get strapped up. Record time. I walked back into the room to find Nina lying on her back fingering herself and alternatively licking her fingers. That made my clit jump like a kid on a trampoline. I crawled between her legs wanting to lick up her juices, but she stopped me.

"This is my time to take control," she said as she flipped me over onto my back.

"I want to ride you and look deep into your eyes as you enter me over and over, going deeper and deeper. I'm in control now, just enjoy the ride," she said as she straddled me.

I watched as she eased my dick inside her. Seeing it disappear and her eyes roll to the back of her head made my clit thump harder than it already was.

"Ooooo," she said, letting out a throaty moan. "Mmmm."

She sat straddling all eight inches of me inside her, allowing herself to adjust to the size. I looked up at her, watching her every move. She was absolutely beautiful. I watched as she slowly began to slide up and down my dick. The way she rotated her hips and rode me was simply hypnotizing. She was a pro. Like I was her prized show horse and she was trying to win the championship. She held my hands, bouncing up and down, kissing me all over my face and neck, whispering taunts in my ear to challenge me. I responded to her taunts by thrusting deep inside her as she slid back down. We crashed into each other over and over until she released my arms. She was riding me with a vengeance, and I wanted her to cum. I needed her to cum. I wrapped my hands around her neck and squeezed as I thrust deeper and harder into her. Ten seconds later her body went stiff, and she started to scream.

"Fuck, Sky!! Yes! Fuck me! Fuck me! Oh, my gawd!!!" she screamed as her body jerked in convulsions. I thrust into her one last time as I watched her body shake on top of me. Finally, she collapsed on top of me, struggling to catch her breath, but I wasn't satisfied yet.

I slid out of her and rolled from under her. She lay face down in the bed. I smacked her ass and watched it jiggle. I leaned down and began to bite her neck and run my tongue up and down her back. She squirmed and moaned. I squeezed her ass cheeks and leaned down to suck and bite them. That made her tuck her legs under herself. She knew what was next. I slid between her legs and spread her ass. I slide my dick up and down her slit to coat it with her juices, occasionally rubbing the head on her clit.

"Please, don't tease me. I want you inside me," she pleaded.

"How bad you want me? Tell me."

"I never knew it could be this good. Fuck me, daddy, and fuck me good," she cried out.

She knew to call me "daddy" drove me crazy. I slid into her slowly and pulled out to the tip. I repeated this motion over and over until she couldn't take it anymore.

"Daddy, fuck me. Don't tease me," she whimpered.

I got into a rhythm and gave her long, deep strokes. She matched each stroke, and we created the perfect silhouette on the wall. The whole scene was intoxicating, and I was drunk off the taste of her left on my tongue, the moans and the smacking of our skin meeting, and the sexy scent that filled the air. I lost all formal control and allowed the sexual beast in me to take over. I grabbed her hips and went deeper and deeper inside her, as I increased speed.

"Yes, daddy. Like that. Oh, shit. Fuck, daddy, I can feel you in my stomach. Harder, baby," she yelled.

Happy to oblige her orders, I wrapped her hair around my hand and pulled it as I thrust harder and harder into her pussy.

"Oh, shit you gonna make me cum again, Sky!"

"Cum for me, baby. Cum all over my dick. Shit, you are so fucking wet."

"Fuck me, daddy! Fuck me, daddy! Fuck me, daddy!"

I released her hair from my grips and grabbed her hips and pounded her pussy relentlessly. I'm sure her pussy would be hurting tomorrow, but it was all worth it.

"Daddy, I'm cumming!!!" was the last thing she said before she let out this high pitched scream and her body went into wild spasms. Three strokes later and I was cumming too. We both collapsed on the bed and I slowly rolled on the side of her, head spinning and mouth hella dry. I laid there for a minute and she looked at me and said: "There's one more thing I want to do before we pass out."

She slid between my legs, took my strap in her hand and began to suck the head. She licked and sucked my dick like a lollipop and as I was watching her in awe, slid two fingers in my pussy and slowly stroked. Her strokes matched those of her sucking my dick. I was losing my mind. I didn't know whether it was from her fingering me or watching her suck me off, but I was quickly approaching a major nut. Just when I was about to tell her to go faster, she deep throated my dick and I lost it.

Her name caught in my throat as the orgasm sent me into seizure-like spasms. The room drifted into a slow spin and I felt my spirit float into another realm. At that moment, our souls become one.

After a few minutes of spiritual elevation, I began to come down from my high and return to the beauty before me. I looked at Nina as she crawled back up to kiss me and lay on my chest. She was my heart, my soul, my everything. Minutes passed with nothing but the sound of our breathing and the smell of sweetness and sex. I could lay here forever.

"I love you," Nina whispered and with that, we fell into a deep sleep in each other's arms—smiles on our faces and souls intertwined forever.

Just You

MyLove Infinitely

I keep replaying the initial moment you slid into my walls. The first gasp of air suspended in my chest. Gentle strokes. One, two, three and slide out. Clitoral stimulation. Tongue rolls from open labia to small circles, soft lips massaging, and you moan on my clit. Anticipation rises. Back arching, hips thrusting down to meet your mouth. Wanting, needing, yearning for you to devour all of me. As the energy begins to shift and my body demands release, with precision you slide in, again. One, two, three strokes—another gasp of air. Waves of euphoric electricity consume every nerve ending in my body.

Breathing heavily with anticipation our bodies collide, rolling me over and positioning on all fours, shoulders down, head tilted. My mind begins to wander, and a new adventure is about to begin.

"Don't move," you instruct.

You get up from the bed and I hear the shuffling of bags and the opening of a box. I'm unable to identify distinctly what is taking place. I try to peak around but it's pitch black. Only the sultry silhouette of my chocolate goddess.

Your voice resonates around the room. "Your curiosity always gets the best of you. Today you will learn. Turn around."

Without hesitation, I oblige. It was something about the command in your tone.

The bed creaks, welcoming your body. Still face down you tenderly caress and rub my back. A strong smack on each cheek delivers chills and my soul becomes weak. I whimper. Both cheeks are spread apart. Gingerly licking your way down my ass, your tongue swirls, invading my hidden box. Nipples hardened as they lay on our soft sheets. My body moistens and a soft moan escapes me. Delving your head deep into my love, it's dripping wet with anticipation. I feel light pressure on my rectum, your thumb at my back door. As you twirl my clit between your tongue and lips, soft shudders course through my body. Hands banging on the headboard, pulling the sheets completely off the bed.

"Fuck," I scream aloud.

I'm so focused on the feelings oozing through every fiber of my body, deliriously unaware that another realm of pleasure is about to begin. Gentle slide in one, two, and three. Another gasp for air.

"Do you trust me?" you ask.

"Yes," is my reply, my tone of voice foreign in this moment.

"Yes, what, my love?" the strong huskiness of your voice meeting the gentleness of my reply.

"Yes, I trust you." In a daze, I am thinking of the next moment but trying to stay in this moment.

"Love, you know I will never hurt you. We are about to go way out of your comfort zone. If at any point you are uncomfortable, you tell me. Do you understand?"

It was in this moment I knew shit had gotten more real.

"Yes," I reply, a quick learner, because clearly, I am not in control anymore. I am being placed in sweet submission.

"Do you want me?"

Thrusting your tongue deep into my gaping vagina, I cry out a yes, damn combo. "What are you trying to do to me?"

With no reply you raise your body, straddling both legs around mine, sliding your fingers into me again. One, two, three, gasp of air. I feel the drizzle of a cool liquid cascading down my opening. And I hear the clicking close of a bottle cap. Spreading the substance across my mound, my thoughts begin to wander But without missing a beat and leaving no room for resistance, you slip the engorged head into my vagina. Crossing the first threshold, my breath is caught in my throat. I slam my hand into the headboard. Adjusting my body, slowly you begin to move this engorged member in and out of my welcoming vagina. Gentle stroke one, two, and three.

"Can you handle more?"

I am only able to shake my head yes to reply. I open up more to you, you give me more, rocking my body into total submission. I feel my orgasm begin to rise and a lubricated finger is slipped into my ass.

"FUCK," I cry out.

Your voice booms around the room. "You cum, my love, and I will stop."

Clenching my muscles down and speaking through gritted teeth, "I can't." You are so in control of this moment and its driving me insane.

Pulling out completely, "You can, and you will, understand? Lay on your back and pull your knees to your chest."

Like a scolded teenager, I pout but turn over. With my legs pulled to my chest, you lean into me. Another dribble of cool liquid, followed by your warm hands. You angle your body over mine. You thrust with pressure sending me over the moon.

"Yes, fuck, shit!' I cry out.

You stroke me slow and deep. I feel myself losing control again.

"What did I say, love? Let's see if you can follow instructions this time."

Shaking my head as my body vibrates in pure bliss. Stroke after stroke, my body gives in to you. Small circles between middle and pointer across my clitoris.

"Don't."

I truly do not know how much of this I can handle but with all the brain power I can muster, I refrain from gripping and begin to meet each thrust. I caress each breast, pulling them together tightly to twirl each nipple. I'm in control now. Noticing the shift in energy, you instruct me to cum. Shit! I grip down on the strap shaft, thrusting forward with each of your strokes. One, two, three. Gasp! My heart beating rapidly, a small bead of sweat trickles down your breast, the intensity in your eyes breaks the dam. Walls tighten and release.

"Good job!"

Slowly, you release me.

Spent, you would think. I admire the work of art before me, a chocolate goddess. Before you think this is over, I slither my way to you. With raised hands you stop me.

"This was all about you, my love. Let it be. I love you."

Switch

Brklyn Vigor

It was clear neither of us needed a shower. Erin smelled of Jean Paul Gaultier's Le Male cologne right behind her ears. I had just taken a shower twenty minutes before she got here. I wanted to be shower fresh. I washed with almond crème body wash and lotioned with the same scented body butter. I grazed my skin with a touch of Kush body oil right below my earlobes on my neck. I was sure she could smell it. It was such a sensual scent. So warm, so enticing. There was no way it could be ignored. That's exactly what I wanted when I saw Erin again. I wanted her full attention. I had it now.

"Tell you what I know?" Erin asked.

"You heard me," I said, biting her earlobe gently after whispering directly into her ear.

I could tell Erin was nervous. She was definitely nothing like what I had heard about masculine women in the bedroom before. Granted, we weren't in the bedroom. I still assumed she would be more aggressive with me at this point. I wondered if I was doing something wrong. Perhaps I was too forward. Maybe it was because I was a bit older. Well, I didn't know how old she was, and I could be assuming. She looked like she could be in her mid-twenties, and I had just turned thirty-one. I was well into what one might say was cougar mode. For Erin's sexy ass though, I didn't give a damn. She was beautiful in her masculinity. She had the curves of a thickly built woman. Voluptuous. She was the complexion of cocoa powder. She was reserved, I could tell from our meeting earlier in the bookstore, but there was a beast lurking behind her eyes waiting to get out. I could see it.

"I thought you said you were supposed to be giving the lesson," she said with a grin, trying to keep water from going into her mouth as she spoke.

I could hear the sarcasm in her voice, as if she thought she had one up on me. I needed her to know that I was still the one running shit. I let my fingers run languidly down her side. I took my time working my way over to her torso and down to her naval. Before she knew it, I was following the sudsy bubbles down her happy trail. I felt her hold her breath as my fingertips got closer to her love, below. Just as she thrust her head back, anticipating pleasure, I slid my palms around her waist and cupped the right side of her ass with a firm grip.

"I didn't ask you who was giving the lesson. You'll get tired of being chastised soon enough, Erin. You must think I like punishing you. Do as I say," I said, looking into her eyes as she bit the side of her lip.

I wasn't usually this bold. I was used to being the one taken advantage of. I was the submissive one generally by default when dealing with more masculine women. The difference with this was, well, I knew Erin wanted me to rough her ass up. I saw the way she flipped through that book on submission in the bookstore. Of course, one could say she was just interested. From the look in her eyes and the way she licked her lips and double backed on a couple of pages though, I knew she wanted her interest to go further than just her imagination. I wanted to be that person to take her on the other side of the game. I wanted to be the one to put her on and turn her out. Who better to do it but me? I was just someone who was as vulnerable in perception, who knew little to nothing about her.

"Let me show you," she said.

She spoke at a volume almost inaudible, which was crazy since we were almost pressed flush against each other. What I did hear was so sexy, though. I'm not sure if it was the way she said it or just what she said. Erin's voice was like a pat of butter on hot grits in the morning—rich and creamy and smooth with a little texture to it. It was slightly raspy. An octave lower than any woman's voice I'd ever heard, but not quite that of a man. Whatever it was, made me just as wet as the shower. I found myself getting ready to submit and letting her have her way with me. I couldn't, though. I needed to stick this out. Make her beg for it. I couldn't lie, partly because I couldn't speak, but she had me weak. I gripped her ass a little harder in lieu of speaking again. If I spoke, my voice would crack, and she'd know she had me.

"Christian, baby, be gentle. Shit." She moaned.

"Tell me what you know," I repeated with a steady voice, luckily.

"I don't know," she lied.

"You don't know? You know something. Bookstore. Sex aisle. Nothing? I don't think so. Come again," I demanded.

"Fine. For starters, I know you've got to make me cum first, before I can come again," she confessed with more aggression in her voice this time.

Before I could act like I was in control of the situation, my body was spun completely around to face the wall where the shower head was. She parted my thighs with one smooth motion of her hand and wrist. It was almost as if I was straddling the knobs to turn on the water. She grabbed both of my wrists and thrust both my arms above my head and pressed them on the shower wall in front of us. I felt the heat of her groin press against my ass and her pubes scratch my skin. My knees buckled. Secretly, this was the moment I craved. God knew how much I wanted to take advantage of Erin and show her that I could run shit, but even more so, I wanted to be at her will. There was no music, but we danced. Our bodies were in sync with a muted rhythm. We went back and forth, forth and back, while our hips went around in a circular winding motion. Her hands expanded from my wrist to my forearms and her body pressed mine up against the tiles on the wall so much that I started to feel the stimulation of my nipples going in and out of the grooves of the tiles. I felt my body slide, slowly, lower and lower down the wall until my groin was grinding on the central knob for the shower. Erin had started to moan and my biceps began to contract and just when I felt my body tense up and my fingers clench on to something that wasn't there, I felt her forearm wrap around my waist and pull my body against her. Water was pouring down our faces but neither of us cared. For a moment no one said anything. She just held me, my back against her torso.

"Since we've established who's really running shit, why don't you show me what you know?" she said into my neck.

I couldn't do shit but moan in agreement. She stepped out of the shower, for what I didn't know. Wish she hadn't left. Wish she hadn't stopped. Part of me was pissed I didn't cum; part of me knew she would make it worth it. I just stood there, trying to gain my composure. I didn't get too far before she was back with a fresh towel in hand, and one wrapped around her waist bare-chested. She smiled slightly and just looked at me. For a moment I forgot I was naked until I saw her eyes wander beyond my face all the way down to my feet. I wanted to be self-conscious. I just didn't have time to.

"You're beautiful," she whispered.

I couldn't do shit in that moment but blush. I didn't know why she was still talking to me like she was on a mission to get the pussy. She made it clear she was in control and my body made it clear it would cooperate.

"Thank you, Erin. You sure know how to make a girl feel good. Really—" I was interrupted with a kiss. Slow. Deep. She kissed with her eyes open.

"Stop talking," she said, draping the towel over my shoulders before she proceeded to dry me off. She pulled me closer to dry my lower extremities then turned me around and dried my back. She got closer to my ass and my body tensed; my back arched, and my ass stuck out. She was strapped up. I could feel her hardness. I turned around to face her to see she had let the towel drop. She pushed my body back against the sink and I instinctively hopped on the counter. She kissed my collar bone, earlobes, neck, and shoulders as I in turn kissed whatever I could reach on her. Before I could focus on what she was doing to me, I found myself gasping and my manicured nails pulling a handful of her locks from the root. I pulled her head back, not necessarily meaning to, but took full advantage of her exposed neck and planted kisses and moans on her skin. She grabbed my ankles, put the bottoms of my feet together, almost like Indian style, and pressed the center of her chest against the sides of my feet facing her for leverage.

"FUCK," was all that came out of my mouth.

There was no effort in that statement, just as there seemed to be no effort in her strokes. She was so fluid with me. She moved like water against my walls. She was quiet. It was as if she was focused on a mission, like she had a goal to reach and a point to prove. I found myself thinking too much about what was behind her eyes and missing out on the moment until she let out a deep moan. She separated my feet, wrapped my legs around her waist, and thoroughly proceeded to knock down my walls. I was expecting her to lose focus of me and concentrate solely on herself when it got that good. She didn't, though. She kept eye contact and matched her breathing and her rhythm with mine until she sped up causing me to make an effort to now match her. She was knocking on the door of the flood gates and my walls were about to come down. She fucked me like she loved me. It was almost like it wasn't a fuck any more at all. The shit was intense.

"Chris, you will not believe the night I had! Girl, I was at the bar and this fine brown papi came—" were the words that fucked up her stroke.

"What the fuck?" she mumbled, looking towards the bathroom door expecting to see someone any minute. She fucked up her rhythm, but oddly enough, she never stopped stroking. My mind was scattered, partly enjoying the feeling of all nine inches of her man-made goodness filling me. The other part of me was waiting in horror for the bathroom door to open.

"Who the hell is that?" she asked, still pounding.

"—into the club up to the bar and—OH SHIT!" he yelled in his falsetto voice.

"Carter," I moaned. She was still going but I could feel her tense up.

"Carter?" she repeated. She was on the verge of cumming.

"ERIN!" I yelled out. It was over. I was done. She moaned, and I watched her body convulse, and for another series of moments we had forgotten about Carter's arrival into the bathroom. Erin finished and kissed me. The sound of

Carter's calfskin leather chocolate boots on the wood floor got her attention. Once again, he acknowledged her confused face, shamelessly.

"Well, damn. Looks like I came just in time. Pun intended," Carter said with a wink. Sometimes I forgot he had an extra key to my pad. Shit.

Angel

Yvonne Moore

[Editor Note: Contains BDSM.]

"She looks like an angel," I think, as I stand across from her in the narrow iron cage.

I watch quietly as curious players make their way around her prison, sliding their hands between the wide bars to caress her with fingertips, feathers, and anything else they think might feel good enough to make her drip with pleasure.

She stands alone, hands cuffed to the ceiling, feet apart and cuffed to the floor of the caressing cage, dressed only in a white lace thong with a silk scarf tied over her eyes, the contrast against her chocolate complexion giving her an air of divinity. Glossy, white bondage tape circles her mouth, taking her speech but failing to stop muffled moans from escaping.

Men and women dressed in as much or as little as they dare engage her remaining senses, stroking her gently and whispering sweet words in her ears as they pass, smiling at one another and admiring her beauty. They regard me with polite gratitude for sharing my angel with them in this world of ours filled with pets and owners, slaves and masters. They take me in as well. My style feminine yet firm, I am dressed in a sheer black teddy, a sexy "peek-a- boo" styled piece that I've chosen to contrast the brightness of her lingerie.

I glance at the clock on the wall. It's been twenty minutes since my angel stepped into the cage, longer than it usually takes for sensory deprivation and captivity to make her weak and wet. She's getting good at this, her confidence allowing her to leave the safety of her comfort zone and discover just how much her body can take.

Another few moments pass before I notice her from the corner of my eye. She is standing before the cage, shyly admiring what she sees, her hands cupped in front of her as she takes in what's happening around her, curiosity and inhibitions dueling in the brightness of her brown doe eyes.

Casually, I stroll to the little doe, smiling my reassurance and taking her hand in mine as I lead her gently closer to the cage. She's shy but willing, my encouragement seeming to waken her bravery.

When we are in front of the cage, I whisper in her ear, giving her permission to touch my angel anywhere not covered in fabric. She reaches for the bars but hesitates, her mind at war with itself, fighting to break the boundaries of what she has been taught to believe is "normal."

I stand behind her, slipping her hand into mine and leading it through the bars. I trace her fingers along my angel's skin, showing her how to make goosebumps rise in their wake. Fear leaves her as she watches my angel writhe and moan under her touch and excitement fills her eyes. I back away, leaving the little doe to her new delight.

Crossing to the locked side of the cage I run my fingers gently across my angel's stomach watching her hands for her response. The thumb of her right hand rises, and I smile. She is ready.

When I reach for the lock, the small crowd backs away and a quiet applause makes a round through the room—a praise offered to my angel for her submission.

I whisper my command in her ear and she grips my hand tightly until she finds her balance, her blindness taking its toll on her equilibrium. I wait for stillness before removing the tape from her mouth. She thanks me, her voice soft and sensual. I feel her trembling.

I tell her she is beautiful, of how well she has done and how proud she has made me. I trigger her reward response knowing that a good dominant is as open handed with praise as they are firm with discipline.

I lead her hand in hand through the crowd of onlookers to the other side of the room, my eyes on the cross as we walk our own road to a very different kind of calvary.

Heavy chains hang from the four points of the wooden "X" shaped apparatus modeled after the one used to martyr the saint whose name it bears.

I lead my angel to the base and back her slowly into position, securing her limbs in the chains until she is again a prisoner to my desire as people start to gather around, eager to see what happens when darkness captures light. The little doe is among them. Our eyes meet and she smiles, igniting an unexpected desire in me to possess her. I extend my hand and motion for her. She breaks from the crowd and comes to me. Again, I walk her to my angel, telling her the rules of engagement, encouraging her to explore however she desires. She follows my lead as we tease my angel in tandem, flooding her senses with erotic stimulation. She moans and jerks beneath us, fighting the urge to run but never speaking the words she knows will make it stop. I kiss her lips as little doe takes a nipple in her mouth, stealing the moan from the air as my angel struggles to stay upright. I step back, moving to the small table on the left side of the cross. I find what I'm after in a small black box, labeled with our name. The crowd watches me as I brandish my prize, a large black vibrator that I turn on high as I make my way back to little doe and my angel. Little doe stops when I reach them. I take her hand and kiss it softly before dismissing her back to the throng of onlookers, her part well played but over.

I turn to my angel running my fingers over her belly again, her body still shaking when her thumb rises . I raise my hand to her neck and squeeze gently until her breathing becomes even and controlled then gliding my hand down her body until I reach the edge of her sex. I pause there for a moment, dancing my fingers across her flesh before slipping them between her legs, moving in circles against her clit. She gasps and moans as I tease her to the edge dipping my fingers inside and drawing more circles until her breathing becomes wild once more, her moans more cry than song.

I turn on the vibrator and step closer, my body pressed to hers as I stroke it against her clit, back and forth until she announces her orgasm to the room. I take her mouth in mine and pull at the scarf on her eyes, restoring her sight as she raises a cry of ecstasy, her body falling into mine as she comes.

When her senses return, she opens her eyes to the room of applauding on-lookers as I release her restraints, holding her by the waist while she struggles to regain her legs.

With our exhibition over, I lead us past broad smiles towards the door where little doe lingers, her hand extended in offering as she waits.

I see her in my bed, her legs draped around my shoulders while I unravel her with my tongue. I see her with my angel doing the same as the sun rises on our hedonism.

My angel moves first, taking her hand and kissing her cheek as they exit together, leaving me to follow their sensual sashay towards our rented room.

I smile slyly, still imagining all the ways I will get to know the little doe.

Intimacy

Marquitta Martin

Lay back slow and let's unwind
Let me squeeze your breast as you squeeze mine
Allow my tongue to kiss your lips below
Until the sweat sets your skin aglow
I hit your G-spot like never before,
Don't try to run while your body I explore
Tantalizing, touching, every bit
Twirling my tongue to explore your clit
I see your eyes roll back, orgasm near
My name you scream for all to hear
I insert my fingers as much as you can take
While eating you like the sweetest of cakes
You came like a waterfall all on my face
And I enjoyed every taste
Now I want to feel you, don't hesitate
Let me see how you reciprocate
I'm so wet and it's because of you
Show me what you got as we start round two

Just Married

Abernathy Ross

[Editor Note: Contains BDSM.]

"Lake Charles is beautiful, isn't it, Addie?" Gio asked, dryly.

"Lake Charles is absolutely stunning, babe. Ten out of ten, would visit again," Adele winked.

Giovanni and Adele had just celebrated their dream wedding in the vibrant and ever lively Big Easy after spending five loving years of dating each other. The second line played "As" while their guests twirled gold and violet handkerchiefs and danced in the street.

The new Mrs. And Mrs. Anderson told their families and friends that they would be spending their honeymoon at the L'Auberge Casino and Resort in Lake Charles, Louisiana. While the women's friends and families were nothing short of supportive and celebrative of their union, the women had used this a cover story for a more, personal honeymoon. The only one who knew differently was Adele's best friend, Marketta, who had to convince the family not to have any flowers or sweet treats sent to a room that didn't exist.

"Are you ready?" Gio asked with a smile, taking her hand into her own. Looking her in the eye, Gio raised their hands together, kissing the back of Adele's. Adele melted. She was a lucky woman, indeed.

"I'm beyond ready," Adele replied, gently rubbing her thumb against Gio's.

The couple excitedly opened the doors of their car, gathering their suitcases and bags and walked up to the door of an apartment they had rented over a travel site. The key, shrouded in black leather, was where the host promised. The women looked at each other, smiling before opening the door to the aptly decorated apartment.

Closing the door behind them, the women exclaimed their awe of the beautifully decorated apartment as they stood and turned in place.

"Whoa, the pictures are great, but this place is even better in person," Gio said, mouth hanging open slightly as she looked around to take everything in.

"You took the words right out of my mouth," Adele replied as she turned to her right, excitedly pointing to a piece of furniture in the other room, "G, baby, there it is!"

Gio turned, looking at what Adele was pointing out in the other room, grinning to herself as she took steps toward the room.

"There it is," she whispered.

The couple walked into the room, flicking the light switch for better lighting. They turned, commenting on the breathtaking array of furniture and décor. The walls of the room were painted a deep sangria, accented with matte black base boards that stood out against the well-kept natural hardwood floors. The center of the ceiling held a gorgeous, small silver chandelier with hanging crystals that sparkled in the light and erotic art of men and women in various BDSM themes that dotted the walls. Gio walked over to the piece of furniture, running her finger down the smooth dark oak of the St. Andrews cross, tapping at the black comfort padding with her fingernail.

Gio bit her bottom lip, eyes still fixed upon the cross. "This is going to be a beautiful honeymoon," she said.

Adele smiled, knowing that this was a long-held fantasy for her wife, "everything feels so surreal right now."

"You ain't never lied," Gio replied with a laugh as she walked over to her wife, taking her hand loosely and twirling Adele into her embrace.

They looked into each other's eyes, taking in one another for a moment before Gio's face showed a salacious smile, slowly curling at the corners of her mouth. Gio wrapped her fingers around Adele's wrist, gently pulling her closer and wrapping her arm around Adele's tiny causing her to inhale sharply.

"I love you," Gio said. Adele's stomach fluttered.

"I love you too, babe."

The women walked out of the main room hand in hand, taking a quick tour of the kitchen and getting a glass of water before gathering their luggage and walking down the hallway toward the bedroom. They looked at each other once more before opening the door, impressed once more with the attention spent to detail. They stepped inside, placing their luggage against the wall as they took in the four-poster canopy style bed with its privacy curtains drawn back.

"I think we need to go shopping," Adele joked, running her hand across the heavy and dark fabric.

The room was meant more for relaxation and aftercare, but still housed features for sexual exploration.

Gio walked over to the bed, inspecting a row of metal rings that were fastened to the post of the bed, "I agree," she said, looking over to her wife and smiling at the inspiration.

Adele walked over to the attached bathroom, opening the heavy wood door and flicking the light switch for better lighting.

"Whoa," Adele said slowly, drawing out the word as she stepped inside the room.

The bathroom, while small, was decorated gorgeously with dark grey tile and a light grout, making the tile stand out against the mauve walls and dark, distressed cabinets with heavy metal fastenings. A distressed, antique looking gothic mirror hung on the wall above the double sink next to a deep red and gold striped fainting chair that sat across from the whirlpool tub with the mauve and black privacy curtain drawn back.

"Yeah, whoa," Gio said, following behind Adele and taking in the lovely furnishing of the room. "It's been a long trip, Mrs. Anderson. Why don't you get washed up and relax for a bit while I put our things away."

"That sounds wonderful, thank you, Mrs. Anderson," Adele replied with a smile, giving her new wife a kiss on the cheek before Gio left the room.

Adele smiled to herself, taking in the emotions and excitement from the day as she undressed, slowly unzipping the back of her mermaid style dress and pulling it down her body. Adele hummed to herself, turning the shiny, metallic knobs of the tub to draw water for her bath. Adele removed her undergarments and set her clothing on the chair, peeking out of the crack in the doorway as Gio started to put away the contents of their luggage.

Adele watched as her just over six-foot wife opened a suitcase, pulling out a plethora of toys and smiling to herself as she laid them out on the bed. *I love her smile*, she thought as she watched Gio run her hand through her curly hair with the undercut Adele loved to play in. Adele smiled, turning back into the room and walking to the tub to run her hand through the warm, inviting water.

Adele stepped into the bath, the water relaxing her as she lowered her body down into the basin. Perfect, she thought to herself with a satisfied smile as she drug her hand across the surface of the water, lightly splashing water against her full breasts. Adele quickly became lost in thought, her mind filled with images of her and Gio putting the various furniture and toys to good use.

Adele turned off the water and leaned back against the basin, running her hand up the dark brown skin of her thigh causing goosebumps to form across her body. Adele closed her eyes, tilting her head back as images of Gio flashed in her mind. She saw her wife above her, her honey brown skin that complimented her determined smile. Adele smiled to herself, her eyes still closed as she slowly ran her hands up her soft, thick thighs and small waist, stopping at her flat stomach just underneath her breasts.

Adele slipped further into the water, biting her bottom lip as she envisioned Gio motioning her to turn over, running her hand slowly up her inner thigh before the sound of her palm connecting with Adele's soft, full bottom, causing her to jump slightly as she gripped at soft, thick fabric. Adele let out a soft moan, running her finger over her folds. I should wait, she thought to herself, wanting to save her first orgasm as a newly married woman for her wife. Adele smiled in anticipation, finishing up her bath and drawing new water to soak for a little longer, the events of the day catching up with her as she started to relax, feeling tired and starting to doze off.

About a half hour later Adele woke, rubbing her eyes as she laughed, a little embarrassed. She lifted herself from the tub, stepping out onto the cool tile floor.

"Aww, babe," Adele said to herself, noticing a fresh set of towels that Gio had laid out for her on the chair.

Adele wrapped her body in the towel and opened the door in the bedroom, noticing a set of white lingerie laid out for her on the dark comforter of the bed with a note:

My princess,
Put this on and come into the living room.

Adele looked around, finding herself alone in the bedroom. And it begins, Adele thought to herself, running her finger down the soft and inviting pristine lace of the lingerie and feeling a familiar tingle between her legs. Adele towel dried her hair and body, putting the towels in a hamper and setting out a fresh set for Gio on the chair in the bathroom if she decided to draw a bath later in the evening. Adele slipped on the lingerie, the crotchless panty exciting her as she fixed the front clasp of the bra, adjusting her breasts for comfort and turning to look at herself in the full-length mirror next to large dresser across from the bed. Damn I look good, Adele thought as she turned from side to side.

Adele walked across the hardwood floor, opening the door and noticing the bright light of the living room illuminating the hallway as she closed the door behind her and made her way quietly down the hall. Just before turning into the living room Adele took another deep breath, smoothing down the lingerie against her skin.

"Come here, Princess," Gio said as she sat in a tall backed leather chair, looking Adele up and down. Legs spread slightly, she looked like she owned the damn place.

Adele smiled, standing still.

"Adele," Gio said in a stern tone.

"Yes?" Adele replied in a cheeky tone, flashing her teeth in a teasing smile as she pivoted on one foot.

"Adele, my love, you know that it is in your best interest to come over here," Gio said with a matter-of-fact tone, resting her chin on top of her interlaced fingers.

Adele smiled, slowly walking over to her wife with a sway in her hips and standing before her. Gio smiled, running her finger down the center of Adele's torso.

"Turn for me my love, I want the full look at the lingerie," Gio said, turning Adele gently by her hip and leaning back to take in the view.

"I love your ass," Gio said, the sound of her palm connecting against the skin of Adele's backside echoing in the room. "It's soft, round, and perfect," she said as she gripped her wife's ample bottom.

"Thank you," Adele said through a quiet, breathy moan, bending slightly at the hips to give Gio a better view.

"I want you to go over to the bench and lay face down," Gio said, running her hand down Adele's back, gently coaxing her toward the bench in the center of the room.

Adele slowly walked over to the bench, running her hand down the leather as she looked back over her shoulder, watching as Gio unbuttoned her suit jacket and placed it on the back of the chair before rolling up the sleeves of her white button-up shirt. Her sleeve tattoo peeked out from underneath.

"On the bench, go on," Gio said with a dimpled smile.

Adele lifted herself onto the bench, turning to lay face down. Adele placed her knees on the leg rests, the position leaving her very exposed.

"Good," Gio cooed, walking around Adele in a slow circle, touching her at random intervals.

"You're welcome," Adele teased, her lips pressing into the leather as she smiled.

Crack!

Adele moaned, the sting of her favorite cat o' nine tails sending bolts of pleasure through her body as she gripped the leather. "You've brought that out early," she said, looking back at Gio with a coy smile.

"It's a special occasion," Gio said with a smile, running the multi tailed whip down Adele's back and bottom, eliciting goosebumps across her wife's supple skin, "have to start this off right."

Crack! Crack!

"That's for being cheeky," Gio said softly, running the leather of the whip between Adele's legs.

Adele moaned, squirming against the bench as her wife teased her. Gio placed the cat o' nine tails on the bench next to Adele's left knee, running her right hand up Adele's inner thigh. Gio cupped her hand over Adele's mound, leaving it there for a moment. Adele squirmed against Gio's hand, moaning out as Gio pressed a finger against her folds, parting them.

"You're quite wet," Gio said, running a slick finger over Adele's sensitive clit.

"You like it, don't you babe," Adele teased, wiggling her hips from side to side.

"Sit. Still." Gio said, firmly, pulling her hand away as Adele whimpered in disappointment.

Gio walked in front of Adele, placing her finger against her lips.

"Lick," Gio said sternly, a smile forming at the corner of her mouth.

Adele lifted her head, looking her wife in the eyes as she opened her mouth and touched her tongue against Gio's finger. Gio bit her bottom lip, watching as Adele lapped at her finger, tasting herself.

"Good," Gio said, pulling her hand away from Adele and walking back behind her, running her hand down her ass, grabbing a meaty handful. "What do you want me to do to you?"

"Want you to make me come," Adele said, pushing back against Gio's hand.

"Mmm, I don't know if you can handle that," Gio replied, pulling her hand back.

"I can handle it baby," Adele replied, wiggling her ass.

"I don't know about that, you always come so quickly," Gio teased, placing her finger on Adele's clit, barely rubbing as her wife moaned, pushing back against her hand. "See, look at you, you can barely handle it right now."

"Try me," Adele said, looking back over her shoulder.

Gio smirked, slipping a finger deep into Adele that elicited a long, loud moan as she moved her finger in a come-hither motion. "See, look at you, I've just started and you're already on the edge. Maybe I should slow down," Gio said.

"No, no please, don't stop, it feels so good," Adele moaned, bucking her hips slightly against Gio's as she felt her insert another finger.

"I enjoy hearing you beg," Gio said softly, removing her fingers and rubbing them against Adele before lightly spanking her pussy.

Gio walked over to the table, picking up a vibrating wand from the table and smiling to herself.

"Come here," Gio said, turning toward Adele.

Adele lifted herself from the bench, smiling at the discarded cat o' nine tails as she stood, smoothing down the lingerie against her body.

"Strip," Gio said, sitting back down in the chair and getting comfortable for the show.

"Aw, but it looks so pretty," Adele pouted.

"Adele."

Adele blushed, walking slowly towards Gio with soft steps. She stopped in front of her wife, running her hands slowly up her body as she turned in place slowly, bending at the waist with her back turned. Adele looked over her shoulder, watching as Gio ran her fingers through her hair, leaning back in the chair with satisfaction.

"Take off your panties, slowly," Gio requested, flipping the wand end over end on the arm of the chair.

Adele bent lower, snapping the band on the thong before pulling the fabric slowly over her buttocks. She moved her hips in an exaggerated motion, pulling the white fabric down her thighs and letting them fall to the floor. Adele pushed the fabric away with her foot, starting to turn but was interrupted by Gio pulling her closer, spreading her legs shoulder width apart.

"Continue," Gio said, pressing the button on the wand and hearing it come to life.

Adele shivered, biting her lip in anticipation. As Adele ran her hands up her sides and breasts, slowly pushing the silky straps of her bra down her shoulder when her body jolted, feeling the vibration of the wand against her thigh.

"Go on, I'm enjoying the strip tease," Gio said with a smile as she pressed the wand head against Adele's pussy.

"Oh fuck," Adele said, trying to concentrate through the constant waves of pleasure.

"Mmm, I enjoy catching you off guard," Gio said, watching Adele shiver and struggle against the vibrations. "Go on, I want to see that bra on the floor," she said, pulling back the wand and turning Adele to face her.

Adele smiled, doing a slow shimmy before opening the front clasp of the bra and covering her breasts with one arm as Gio placed the wand back against her. Adele pressed against the wand, looking Gio in the eyes as she slowly pulled the fabric away from her skin, dangling it on the end of her finger with little jolts of her body before letting it fall to the floor.

"Put your arm down," Gio said, pressing the wand against her a little harder, turning up the vibration.

Adele yelped in surprise, rocking her hips against the wand as she tilted her head back and slowly dropped her arm to reveal her breasts. Gio leaned forward, keeping the wand in place as she ran a finger around Adele's hardened nipples. Adele felt on the cusp of orgasm, trying to hold back as she started to exhale and moan rapidly.

Click.

"See, told you. You were already on the edge," Gio said teasingly as she stood, leading Adele over to the St. Andrews cross.

Adele took a deep breath, not knowing what to expect but was excited to experience the paces her wife would put her through. Gio kissed Adele passionately, backing her up against the wood and leather and raising her wife's arms above her head, strapping each arm in place. Adele smiled, baring her teeth in excitement as Gio pushed her legs apart, strapping each ankle in place and slowly running her hand up her wife's body, stopping at her breasts.

Gio lightly flicked and pinched at Adele's nipples, causing her to tug against the restraints. She bent slightly, her mouth level against her wife's nipples. Gio flicked her tongue against the hardened buds, watching and listening as Adele moaned and pushed against the leather bindings before moving down onto her knees. Gio looked up, watching Adele breathe heavily.

"Please baby, please make me come," Adele said through heavy breaths as she pushed out her hips.

"All in due time my love," Gio murmured, lightly raking her fingertips against the insides Adele's thighs causing her to squirm and laugh from the ticklish sensation.

Gio smiled, leaning her body forward and teasing Adele with her breath before pressing her tongue against Adele, licking and lapping against her clit. Adele moaned loudly, clenching her fists and rocking her hips against Gio's face. She smiled, relishing in the movements and sounds coming from Adele.

"Don't stop baby, please don't stop," Adele moaned through her teeth, pressing the back of her head against the smooth leather headrest of the St. Andrews cross.

Gio moaned against Adele, placing her hand against her right calf just underneath Adele's peacock tattoo for better leverage. Gio penetrated Adele with her tongue, enjoying the taste as Adele bucked against her mouth. Gio moved her hands to lightly grips Adele's hips, pressing her back against the cross in place as she flattened her tongue against her slickness. Delicious. Gio took Adele's pussy into her mouth, gently sucking and running her teeth across delicate skin as she pulled her mouth back, looking up at her wife with a confident smile.

Adele took heavy, shuddering breaths, watching as Gio stood and walked over to the table and removed the rest of her clothing. She smiled, her eyes moving from the soft skin of her broad shoulders, to her heavy breasts and then down to her lovely, muscular legs. That's my...wife, Adele thought to herself, the day still feeling surreal. That's all mine.

"What is that look for?" Gio asked, picking up a strap from the table and stepping into it before turning to face Adele.

"You cute," Adele replied with a wink. "Are you single?"

Gio laughed. "I'm single, but this wife of mine..." Trailing off, she returned to Adele. Pressing her body against hers, rubbing the PVC phallus against her. Gio grasped the base as she passionately kissed Adele, rubbing the toy against Adele's opening as their tongues and lips intermingled with each other. Gio pressed her pelvis forward, feeling a little resistance before the toy slipped deep into her wife, causing Adele to moan into her mouth.

Gio smiled, gently nipping Adele's lip as she rocked her hips in a slow, repetitive motion. Adele gripped at the tops of the binding, her moans increasing in volume as Gio's pace hastened.

"Ahh, don't stop!"

Gio abruptly stopped, quirking an eyebrow at the demand that drew a whimper from Adele.

"Just kidding," Gio said with a smile as she gripped Adele's hips, catching her off-guard as she thrust hard.

Gio threw her head back, moaning as she enjoyed the sensation of the toy rubbing against her sensitive clit coupled with the sounds and movements coming from her wife. Gio didn't let up, quickening her pace further to drive Adele over the edge.

"Yes daddy, fuck me, please make me come," Adele moaned, feeling herself quickly reaching the edge.

Gio growled loving it when she worked Adele into enough of a frenzy to call her daddy. She gripped Adele's hips harder, her eyes fixed on her wife's face as she fucked her as hard as she could. Gio continued to watch, enjoying the sounds fill her ears as Adele's face contorted with the initial crash of the tidal wave of pleasure.

"Yes daddy, yes! Don't stop, I'm coming, I'm coming!" Adele moaned, her words turning into a low, guttural growl that was broken with each of Gio's hard, deep thrusts.

Gio continued to thrust, the building of her own orgasm peaking as she ran her hands up Adele's sides, cupping her breasts. Gio pressed her lips to Adele's, moaning into her mouth as she fell over the edge, each thrust feeling as if her cells were lit aflame with pure ecstasy.

Adele and Gio stood in place, breathing heavily as they savored the moment. Gio pulled her body back, the sensation of the strap slipping out of Adele causing her to shiver and moan.

"My, my, my. You're still very sensitive," Gio said, smiling as she lightly rubbed Adele's clit, causing her body to jerk from the sensation overload.

Gio released the bindings from Adele's wrists and ankles, giving her a moment to collect herself as she walked over to the table, removing the strap and placing it on the table. "You good?" she asked with a grin.

Adele looked at Gio, a dumbfounded look on her face before chuckling, "you have to ask?"

"What?" Gio laughed, "everyone loves a good ego stroke."

They laughed, walking into the kitchen for a glass of water as they talked about their session together before deciding to turn in for the night, the days events and first session together as newlyweds catching up to them. Gio picked up Adele, holding her close as she turned off the light and walked them into the bedroom.

Gio retrieved a pair of boxer briefs and sports bra from her luggage, walking over to the bathroom and turning on the light as Adele prepped for bed.

"I'm going to wash up, I won't be long," Gio said, kissing Adele.

"No problem love, I'll be here, I just can't guarantee I'll be awake when you get out," Adele replied with a soft chuckle, stretching her arms behind her.

Adele retrieved her own sleepwear, a matching lilac tank top and shorts that were soft and silky to the touch and slipping them on. She walked over to the bed, drawing back the comforter and lifting herself on the bed. She luxuriated in the soft and welcoming blankets, laying back and adjusting the pillows as she smiled to herself, pleasantly overwhelmed with the events of the day and evening as she slowly drifted off to sleep, making good on her word to Gio.

Adele stirred, slowly opening her eyes as she woke early in the morning. She listened to the birds as she rolled onto her back and turned to head towards Gio who was still asleep. Adele smiled to herself, listening to Gio's cute, quiet snores. She rolled back over, grabbing her phone to make sure she didn't miss any important calls before getting up and quietly walking over to Gio's side of the bed, checking to make sure she didn't have any important notifications of her own.

Adele slowly drew back the comforter, smiling to find that her wife had decided to sleep in the nude after all. Thank you baby, she thought, slowly positioning herself between Gio's legs, causing her to lightly stir. Adele kissed at Gio's face and lips, gently coaxing her from her slumber.

"Good morning my love," Adele said, smiling before slowly kissing down Gio's neck and shoulders.

"Good morning indeed," Gio replied, cupping the side of Adele's face and rubbing her thumb on her cheek.

Adele continued to plant tiny kisses, stopping at Gio's breasts. She cupped her left breast, rubbing her thumb over Gio's hardening nipple as she flicked her tongue against the left, smiling as Gio let out a soft grunt. Adele continued to kiss down Gio's torso, moving down Gio's body before pushing her legs up and parting them.

Adele looked up, watching as Gio smiled, sharply sucking air through her teeth as she kissed down her pubic mound and quickly pressed a kiss Gio's clit. Gio raised her hips impatiently, and Adele smiled against the inside of her thighs. She gave each one loving attention with teeth and tongue that would make Gio think of her anytime she pressed her thighs together. Gio gave her a look that firmly said "don't play," but Adele smirked, and gave her another hickey to match the one she had left on the right. She reveled at the way Gio's chest rose and fell hard, watching her work. Teasing the wet slit with the back of her finger, she chuckled as Gio let out a grunt of frustration.

Adele wrapped her arms around blessedly thick thighs as she pressed her lips against Gio, teasing her with hot breaths. Adele kissed, extending her tongue and flicking it against Gio's clit, before running it up and down her swollen lips. She shook her head, the sensation causing Gio to grip the sheets with one hand and place the other on the back of Adele's head, gripping her hair.

"You're fucking killing me," she said, with a pained laugh.

Adele smiled, tilting her head to one side as she continued to flick her tongue and move her hand to lightly rub her thumb against Gio before placing her palm against her mound. Adele pressed Gio's mound back slightly, giving her better access to her clit, watching for a moment as it throbbed before pressing her mouth against it and circling her tongue, causing Gio to moan louder and grip her hair harder. Her hips rocked forward, stealing as much control as Adele would allow her, until she was fucking Adele's mouth.

Adele continued to circle her tongue, gently sucking and kissing at random intervals as she moved her hand, parting Gio's slick folds with her finger and slowly pressing one then two slowly into her and then turning her hand palm up. Gio moaned and gently rocked her hips against Adele's fingers, reveling in the slowly building pressure as Adele picked up pace.

Gio looked down at Adele, feeling her pull her mouth away as she kissed at her inner thigh, right against the hickey already starting to form, hearing a soft "oh, *shit*" for her efforts.

There's nothing Adele loved more than making Gio cuss in bed.

Adele quirked an eyebrow at her wife before pressing her lips firmly against Gio's skin, taking some into her mouth and sucking as she continued to pump her fingers. Gio moaned, tilting her head back and closing her eyes as she gasped.

Adele continued to suck, pulling back her lips after about a half a minute, admiring the hickey she left behind before pressing her mouth back against Gio's pussy, flicking and dragging her tongue over Gio's sensitive flesh. Gio rocked her hips harder, her body jolting at times as the pressure built and built.

Adele smiled, intensifying her motions as Gio pulled her closer, letting out one last strangled moan as she came. As Gio shivered from the aftershocks, Adele lapped up every drop. Dragging her tongue back up to the swollen bud, she brought her wife to another climax before releasing her with a soft pop.

Gio, once recovered, would make her pay dearly for that. They hadn't pulled out the blindfold, yet, after all, and the room was theirs for one more night. She looked forward to making it to good use.

Adele pulled her body back, looking up at her wife with a smile, "You good?" she said with a laugh.

Gio smiled, pulling Adele up to her, kissing her, "uh, yeah, and the hickeys were the icing on the cake."

"I thought it was pretty hot," Adele said, kissing the end of Gio's nose.

"Very hot indeed," Gio replied, laying back to catch her breath as Adele settled into the crook of Gio's arm.

"I love you," Adele said softly, "so, so much."

"I love you too," Gio said, rubbing her thumb against Adele's hip.

Gold

Nyx

The gold in her eyes
Pulls me in
And when I think,
When I think
I'm about to drown
And all is lost for me
Smokey, wispy lashes close
And open again
And I am released,
Only,
To be pulled back into
the deep undercurrent below
That continuously pulls me in
Deeper and deeper
Every time.

Portrait of Love

Angel Mystique

Two blank canvases

That developed into a visual landscape of emotional hues

Overlooking the doubts in my mind.

You give me an intense sense of calmness,

Too deep for single flowers to grow

But nurturing fields that are easy to find.

Leading me on a journey unsure to take

Sensual stagnation had me afraid

As our closeness removes time.

Having thoughts of losing this moment

Your eyes promise peace and compassion

Our kindred souls allow me to trust.

Climbing out of this loneliness

My imaginative mind won't leave behind

As we're led by a simple

Portrait of untouchable Love

...between us.

Do What You Feel

Amor Jomei

Sometimes I fantasize

Fantasize about you

Taking me to levels unimaginable

Depths, so unknown

Hearing screams and moans

Not realizing they're my own

I dream about your lips

Seductively licking them before sending them down my back

Leaving trails of your softness to tickle my spots

I imagine you kissing the back of my neck

Silently writing your name with the tip of your tongue

Creating electric shocks up and down my spine

Struggling to control my body

Turning me over

Playfully brushing your lips over mine

Gazing deeply into my eyes

I reach out to kiss you

But you slap my hand away

Tonight, you run the show

Wanting total control

You tie my hands to the bedposts

"I want to enjoy you in every way tonight

No objections or attempts to escape," you say

Giving you a devilish grin, I whisper, "Do what you feel"

You slowly kiss me

Making love to my mouth

Kissing your way down my neck to my chest

Drawing circles around my nipples before engulfing them in your warm mouth

Mmmmm! It feels so good

Attention! As the other nipple salutes you

Silently begging for you to play with her too

As if you read her mind

You take her in your fingers and begin to massage life into her

After playing with the twins for a while

You travel farther south

Stopping to kiss my navel

Planting kisses all over my stomach

You continue your trail into the valley

Carefully spreading my legs

Making yourself comfortable

You lick up and down my thighs

Teasing me terribly

Getting just close enough for me to feel your presence

Only to pull back

You kiss my lips

Never once exploring between them

I'm squirming

Anticipating the moment you dive in

You slide your fingers between my lips

Dipping slowly into my honey pot

I bite my lip and release a deep moan

You begin to slowly pump your fingers

In and out

Rotating my hips to meet your thrusts

You take your fingers out and place them in your mouth

Slowly licking my juices off while staring directly into my eyes

That drives me crazy

"Baby, please taste me

I need to feel you," I moan

Just like that, you wrap my legs around your shoulders

I part my lips and you begin to flick your tongue on my clit

Running your tongue up and down my pearl

I'm moaning for you to lick harder

Lick faster

You start to suck the life out of my pearl

I'm struggling to move away

It feels so good

Wishing I could grab your head

I moan your name

"I'm going to cum"

You lick and suck my pussy like you've been walking in the desert all-day

And I'm your first drip-drop of water

I'm screaming your name

Begging you to stop

Needless to say, you don't

Instead, you keep going as my walls come crashing down

Sending my body into convulsions

I don't know what's gotten into you, but you don't stop there

Tears roll down my face as you bring me to yet another shattering orgasm

I want to fuck you so bad at this point

But you obviously have other plans in mind

You get up and give me a deep, passionate kiss

The taste of my juices lingering on your tongue and lips adds to my excitement
    You break away and tell me the fun isn't over yet
    You disappear into the bathroom
    Leaving me lost and confused, wondering what could be next
    "Can you handle it?" I hear you say
    Turning my head, I see you holding my strap and honey
    You walk to the bed with a wicked smile spread across your face
    You strap me up and pour holding it down
    Slowly you began to lick and suck my strap
    You pinch my clit as you deep throat the entire strap
    That sends me over the edge...again
    After licking up all my juices, you untie my hands and lay next to me
    Looking me straight in my eyes, you say
    "You can make me cum now."

Regards, My Dear

L.M. Bennett

The first time they met was when Wil delivered the new desktop tower. She rushed through the introduction, but Wilhelmina "Call Me Wil" Briggs was the tech who would be assisting her today. Thayer had noticed how the taller woman appeared to look away too quickly when their eyes met, but IT people weren't the most deft at basic social interactions, so she thought nothing of it.

But then they both reached for the mouse at the same time, Wil's warm hand covering hers for a hot second, and this time it was Thayer pulling away as if she had been burned, the heat from that single, accidental touch creeping up into her cheeks. Before her head snapped back to the screen, she caught Wil looking down, a pair of dark lashes fluttering against dimpled cheeks, and she swallowed hard.

"I've got to go...get a part," Wil said, looking startled. "Just a...yeah. I'll be back."

"Okay," Thayer said, nodding dumbly.

Wil didn't come back. Not for the rest of the day, or the day after, not even when Thayer put in a ticket for something she already knew how to fix. When Dorky Donny arrived at her desk that afternoon instead of Wil, she forced a smile and sat through his fumbling around her computer. The cherry on the top of all that was when she saw Wil an hour later, hunched over Jaleesah's computer, saying something to make her laugh and tuck her braids behind her ear. Of all people. She had half a mind to tell Cyn about her fiancée...smiling at other people...who are attractive. But that would open up wounds she had finally learned to stop picking at, and that was a no.

Focus, Thayer.

Not that Wil was hot in a classical sense, or anything. Sure, she had big kewpie doll eyes, broad nose and apple cheekbones, and there was the way her lips rested above a chin that, when she smiled, made her face look like a heart. Or something. If you liked that sort of thing. But then there was the slight thickness she had which was evident under her fitted blue polo and khakis. Tall, with broad shoulders, and long fingers at the end of veiny arms, which probably would feel amazing and huge against her lower back, pushing her down, making her arch deeper, and—holy fuck, okay, *now* she was staring.

Wil must have sensed someone looking at her, and when she locked eyes with Thayer, her smile faltered for a bit as her cheeks reddened. Bundle of nerves, patting the back of her head. The heat was back at Thayer's cheeks, probably making them as red as her shoes. Thayer looked away first. Dammit. When she gathered the nerve to glance back, Wil was still looking at her, mouth slightly agape.

Thankfully, her phone rang, snapping her out of whatever thoughts she was having at that moment, which did NOT include kissing, or biting lips or looking into eyes of any sort.

There was absolute radio silence for a few days, including a holiday weekend she used for Law & Order, unlimited kitty snuggles in place of Oreos and engaging in general pantlessness and a lack of human interaction. A blessedly serene three-day weekend in which she did not think about cuddling thick, brown-skinned girls with messy 'fros at all. Much. Often. Whatever. Then, on Tuesday, things started breaking at her desk. Failed software updates. Password issues. Things that should not have been broken in the first place, for which she would have to put in a ticket to have fixed.

And, like clockwork, here would come Wil to fix them. Each and every time. Crowding her space with a shy grin, having the nerve to smell and look like the very snacks she deprived herself of at home, and she was starving. On Thursday,

Thayer had offered to get up out of the chair so Wil could re-orient the landscape on her monitor, but Wil insisted on leaning over her instead. Thayer fought to keep her breath even and her eyes from going half-lidded as Wil pressed against her back.

After she got locked out of the company inventory software in the middle of a pretty fucking important call, she started to put in a ticket, but got a better idea. Walking as fast as four-inch heels and a pencil skirt would let her, Thayer marched over to Jaleesah's desk, where she was probably boring Wil to tears with some story about wedding planning. She deliberately ignored the picture of Jaleesah and Cyn at the Eiffel Tower, training her gaze squarely on Wil.

"Yes," Thayer said, simply.

"—excuse, me, Thayer, can I help you...?" Jaleesah asked, in a tone of voice which was stunningly condescending, even for Jaleesah. Neither woman acknowledged her.

"—What?" Wil looked puzzled, much in the way that the killer on Law & Order knows what he's about to be questioned for, before Lennie has even fixed his mouth to make a wiseass comment.

"Yes, I will go out with you. Now do you think you could please stop breaking things?!"

"You knew?" Wil said later on that evening, leaning over her plate, the taco dipping sauces ignored for now. It might have been the lingering effects of the lime margarita shot, but for the first time Thayer noticed how the flickering candlelight brought out how brown Wil's eyes were. Not black like her own, but actual warm, chocolate orbs that she wanted to dive into. Brown like the mole sauce Wil had snuck a spoonful of earlier in the night, flicking away the remnants from the corner of her mouth with her tongue.

Thayer leaned in across the table, ostensibly to get a better look, and she could see Wil sucking in a breath. Wil's hand was covering one of her own on the table, fingers curled as if a warning. Thayer smirked at that, her other hand seeking the rim of her glass for the lime. This would be one for the ages, she thought.

Fixing Wil with her most lethal stare, she placed the lime to Wil's mouth.

You Touched Me

Unique Lee

You
  touched me
  touch me still
  making rise
  passion
  like lustfully sucked
  lips
  down my spine
  run chills
  causing me to quiver
  under the weight of your body
  between my thighs
  spreading
  over me
  my skin
  your breath
  hot
  spreading over my skin
  quivering
  I cling to you

nails in your back
I cling to you for dear life
for something real
something stable and strong
to steady me
as you touch me
'cause I'm quivering
and you're moaning
'cause your flesh opens
and I open
and minds open
and hearts open
yes, mine opened
as your lips parted
feverishly - hungrily - carnally
your hand at my throat
forcing my face up
and over yours
then away
then away with yesterday's fears and inhibitions
slipping away like love's melody
through my parted lips
as my hips
part
and again the quivering starts
our hearts pounding
to the rhythm of the headboard
rocking
and rolling
over each other
with roughly disciplined fervor
that sends sweat pouring

like a waterfall
gushing
between us
both
hungry for more
yes, more
quivering and clinging and opening
and wanting more
like that first lick
of the sweetest thing
that tickles the tongue
and satiates taste buds
but there's nothing to quench this thirst
no
more
I'm ravenous now for more
like heroin
I need you flowing into me
ev-er-y day
through me
till I'm quivering
for more
feenin'
blowing up your crackberry
pipe
that you been layin' down
up in here
and here and here and oops
you're not ready for more yet?
'cuz I'm quivering
where
you touched me.

Desire (The Fire)

Queen Uni

I see you smile,
>It warms my heart.
>I touch your skin,
>It warms my heart.
>You touch my skin,
>Call me beautiful,
>I smile and I kiss your lips.
>Lips so soft,
>Lips so gentle.
>A kiss that feels like it will last,
>Night after night,
>I can't resist,
>Putting my hands,
>All over you.
>Touching you with all of me,
>Scratching your back,
>And knowing how it makes your insides fire.
>Firing my insides,
>Hearing your breath race,
>Knowing that you're excited,

Turning me on with you,

Turning me on inside of you,

Turning you on with me,

Turning you on inside of me,

Kissing you harder, kissing you as if these kisses can

Take me to what I feel inside these flames of desire.

Tongues flaring up, together, running together, chasing each other,

Hands running along skin,

Quicker, faster,

Desire overtaking any other feeling,

Just desire inflaming that inner flame.

Overtaking,

Sweet kisses,

Into sexy ones.

Gentle touches,

To arousing ones.

Smiles fading, kisses deepening,

Hands running along every inch of skin.

Every inch.

Open arms, open clothes, open hearts, open.

Thigh meeting with thigh, lips pressed to lips,

hands intertwined with hands, bodies nude,

stripped of everything except desire,

the growing flame.

The flame overtakes everything.

One last scratch, and you arch and gasp,

my fingers run from the edge of your back.

Graze to the front of your stomach,

Trail across the outer lips of your vulva,

Over the wet place of your beautiful pearl.

I stroke you, you squeeze me, I gasp, you kiss me.

I stroke you, you squeeze, you gasp, you breathe.

I continue to pleasure you.

I watch the flame of desire rise all over your skin,

feel it burn all over my skin,

skin kissing skin, skin rubbing skin,

your fingers dance along my clit.

I look you in the eyes and my fingers warm deep inside of you.

You moan with pleasure, you cry with pleasure, pleasure.

So much pleasure.

I watch as your flame of desire bursts and you moan, gasp, and nearly scream.

I bring you closer,

You set my desire to burst, and you watch as I cry out your name with extreme passion,

You bring me closer.

I close my eyes,

You close your eyes,

We seal the passion with a kiss.

I open my eyes,

You open your eyes,

I see you smile,

It warms my heart.

Break from the Ordinary

Daydreamer

[Editor Note: Contains Hard BDSM.]

I put the keys into the lock and turn until I hear the familiar click heralding my arrival. It was the same routine. I enter the house as I normally did, quiet, so as not to wake its inhabitants. I place the keys in their spot in the china cabinet, second shelf, in the purple and ivory plate, sure that I would remember where they were in the morning. Same place.

Sigh.

I stop short, feeling unusually restless this evening. I'm noticing everything lately has been the same routine. Get up, go to work, and come home, in the exact same order...I walk slowly to the bedroom, careful not to make too much noise. I wouldn't want to wake the children. As I reach the bedroom, I realize that you are asleep. I stand there, leaning against the edge of the door, staring at you. You are lying on the bed, head slightly underneath the pillow. Your hair is slightly damp from sweating in your sleep. Your right arm is above your head, while your left arm covers your body, with your fingers tucked slightly inside the waist of your pajamas.

As I stare at you, my fingers start to roam over my breasts. I can feel my nipples start to harden under the white blouse I'm wearing. Fingertips continue to travel, lightly caressing my side on the way down my suit pants to land directly atop my clit. I can feel the throbbing and the temperature rising. As I remove my blazer, eyes never leaving your body, I realize I am hungry. Not that "I haven't eaten all day" hunger, but the guttural instinct to mate. I realize that it is time for a break in routine. I am hungry for you.

I move toward the bed, slowly, an animal stalking its prey.

Suddenly, I am straddled on top of you, hand around your throat, loving the startled gasp that escapes you. My hand closes tighter as your eyes begin to focus and you realize that it is me. Your heart beating fast as you struggle to sit up, and faster as you realize you can't. I love the look of wonder, curiosity, and fear in your gaze as you look into my eyes.

"I'm hungry."

It's all I can say without letting the growl escape. I see your nipples harden and feel the beginning of a sigh building in your throat. I loosen my grip momentarily...just long enough to hear you whisper, "Yes, Mistress."

The way your body arches up to mine, the look in your eyes, is driving me crazy. I want to claw you and taste you from head to toe. The smell of strawberries gets stronger as your passion begins to rise.

"Strip."

It is not a request. As I release my hold on your neck and move from atop your body, you slowly begin removing items of clothing. I watch as you removed the t-shirt that clung tightly to you. I moan as your hips lifted from the bed to remove the pajama pants that seemed to flow with the movements of your body. As much as I enjoy watching, my mind is ten moves ahead picturing all the things I want to do to you.

With a speed I didn't realize I had, I am straddling you again. Completely naked, skin against skin, I can feel your body rub against my pussy. Strangely, I don't remember taking my clothes off.

"Shhhh." Finger to my lips, I order you to be quiet. No other words spoken. Yet I know you can feel the urgency and need emanating from me.

I stare at you as my hands roam over your body. Every touch causes a reaction and every reaction causing my guttural instincts to take over a bit more. I caress your arms with my fingertips, making sure to graze the tip of my nails over soft spots prone to exciting you. I use my pointer finger to urge your mouth open slightly. You oblige, letting a solitary moan escape you.

I insert my thumb into your mouth, running my nail against your tongue. Watching with a smile as you roll your tongue around the tip. You try to close your eyes, but a firm grip on your chin makes them open once more.

"Good girl."

As I move my thumb from your mouth, down your chin, to your throat, I lean forward slowly to lick your tongue. I love swallowing the moan as you feel my thumb press into the hollow of your throat.

"Time to get you wet."

You follow me from the bedroom to the shower. Still dazed from being awakened so abruptly, you stumble a little, trying to get your balance as you struggled to keep up. As I turn the light on, you close the door and open your mouth to speak.

I don't think you saw it coming. The slap to your face was fast and hard. Shock shone in your eyes and a moan would have escaped but at that moment you saw me with my finger to my lips, the stern look on my face.

"Shhh."

We get into the shower. You stand there awaiting your next order as I lean forward to turn the knob. My eyes never leave you. I can see your urge to question, the need to speak strong. Then the water hits your body in a sudden burst of spray. As the hot water streams down on us, I grab a fist full of your hair and I pull you to me for a kiss. Inhaling your scent as I lean closer, my eyes roll upward into my head at the pure aroma of your heat combined with the steam of the water hitting your skin. I trace the outline of your lips with my tongue. I ravish your mouth until neither of us could breathe. I watch as you bite your lip, panting. You look at my lips expectantly, almost begging me to give you one more kiss.

I lean closer, hand still buried in your hair, fist tightening, and I yank backward as my teeth take hold of your bottom lip and I pull in the opposite direction. I hear you moan as you resist my fierce hunger. I can taste blood as my teeth cut into your lip. Mmmmm....

It excites me. A low growl erupts from me and I bite harder. More blood trails from between our lips and my tongue anxiously follows. I taste iron as I lap at the red streams, feeling you shudder from the sensation of tongue on chin beneath hot water, along with the sting from the opening in your lip where my teeth had been. Oblivious to the water continuing to flow down onto us, I turn you around and thrust you against the wall. With one hand still in your hair, the nails of my other hand follow the trail of droplets down your back. Slowly and deliberately, my nails dig deeper into you. The water on the fresh scrapes stinging, eliciting hushed moans from you. Forcefully, I press my body to yours, aching for you as my breasts rub against your back; nipples hardening as my pussy nears your ass.

Finally, I release your hair, using both hands to firmly grasp your ass and lift, causing you to lean further, harder against the shower wall. Quickly, I take one hand and reach beneath you, using the tip of one nail to trace an invisible line from the tip of your clit backward, to the base of your ass.

I love the slight jump you give me. Yet it earns you a slap to your ass and a hard shove against the wall. Both hands reach up to your neck. You feel my nails raking from your chin downward as you hear the metal clank of the collar being clasped around your neck. A shiver rocks your body and I grin. The leather of the collar is cold against your hot skin. I can feel your urge to touch the collar...to run your fingers over the single metal ring positioned deliberately at the center of your throat. You fight the urge, but you want to touch badly.

I turn you towards me so that I can see the cloudy look in your eyes. You are alternating between biting your lip and tracing them with your tongue. Your eyes are glued to my lips.

"Kiss me."

It is barely a whisper and I could scarcely believe I heard it.

"Say it again, sweet one." The statement is low, almost a whisper. You open your mouth to repeat and reel back with the force of the slap I gave you. My palm connects firmly with the line of your jaw. The sting, the force, and the pleasure from it, all surprising you as you taste blood. A soft cry escapes you and I force you to look me in the eye as once again, my finger is at my lips.

"Shhh."

As our gazes held, I lift the blindfold to your face. It's no more than a ribbon. It's thick enough so that no images could seep through and wide enough that it covers just a little more than your eyes. Satin with lace trimming, I'd picked it out for you just last week. You didn't know, but I was saving it for a special occasion. I think this is a special occasion. Your eyes never leave mine. You can see every emotion, every need play across my face. Then suddenly, you were a slave to your emotions. I fasten it tight around your head. Shrouded in darkness, you can't see me. All you could do was to wait, anticipate, and enjoy.

Gliding my palm gently over your face as my hands find their pathway downward to your wrists, you gasp as you hear cuffs lock in place. Cold metal, tight at your wrists and it was killing you not to be able to see their design. It frustrates you to know that you can't see exactly what binds you. You are completely helpless, and as you realize this, another shudder.

"It's time to have some fun." The smile is bright on my face and I wait expectantly.

"Yes, Mistress."

I turn the water off and lead you from the shower by the chain. Slowly, we walk down the darkened hallway. Carefully, I lead you so as not to wake the children. I can hear the slight indrawn breaths that escape you. In the quiet of the house, I could even hear the water hitting the floor as it dripped from every part of your body. Again, I smile. I take you to the dining room.

"Give me your hand."

You raise your hand slowly and I place the chain in your hand as I turn to move the table backward. I move it far enough so that I can chain you to the hook directly in the center of the room. Scraping noises assault your ears and you crane your head as if you could actually see what I was doing. I turn toward you once more and stare at you for a second.

The room is dark except for the moonlight streaming into the windows. Just enough light to cast an eerie glow over your body and illuminate the table. You are dripping wet. Steam and droplets of water fall from you as your body temperature adjusts from the sudden change in climate. You are trembling, legs together, and one hand at your side, the other holding the chain extended outward. I stare at the place your eyes should be, and though blind-folded, it's like you could feel my gaze and at the instant realization, you drop your head.

"Bring it to me."

"Yes, Mistress."

You walk forward in darkness. Trying to walk a path for the place you guess I'd be, attempting not to show the shakiness in your step. You know the house well, though. You find me with a start, almost as if you didn't expect it would be so easy. You place the chain in my hand, and I reach upward putting it firmly in its place.

Your arms above your head, head slightly leaned back, blindfold tightly covering your eyes, and your ass slightly touching the table, I am ready to begin my exploration. I walk in semi-circles slowly around you, hanging there. The table hinders me from going in a complete orb around you, but I want it that way. I am far enough away so that you cannot tell exactly where I am, but close enough that you can feel the ferocity building in me. The longer I stare at your body prone, helpless, before me, the more animalistic I become.

I feel the gentleness leaving me as I run a stray nail down the center of your body, stopping to trace a circle around your naval. Your stomach shivers as the edge of my nail whispers across; a completely involuntary reaction.

Your body reacts to me. I can feel my own excitement, my pussy wet from how your body moves. Wanting to lean closer, to urge me to touch more, your restraints hold you in place. I continue...almost pacing the same invisible arc around your body, wanting to dig my teeth into you ravenously, but fighting the urge, wanting to savor the moment.

A low guttural growl escapes me. I can see the shudder as it ripples through your body. I can imagine the thoughts in your head as you wonder what I will do next. I can't help myself. My right hand shoots out and rakes a line across your belly. You gasp and before you complete the indrawn breath, the other hand follows the first, downward across your shoulders and breast. More ragged breaths escape you and they hiss out as my nails leave your body, only the sting reminding you where they had been moments before.

I move closer to sniff the crook of your neck. Of its own accord, my tongue snakes out to lick your chin.

Mmmmm.

Quickly following my tongue, my nail goes right to the soft place beneath your chin as I whisper a kiss across your lips. Still wet from the shower, slightly apart, I can feel them tremble and purse in anticipation.

As my lips press more firmly against yours, my arms reach behind you to claw your back. They dig firmly into you and retreat slowly, returning to their starting place but not before opening a doorway for the blood to freely flow. You tense at the invasion into your body, yet you sway into me from the pure pleasure of it. I can feel the wetness of the blood against my fingertips. Rubbing my fingers over the open wounds, I ensure that my fingers are covered in your blood, your essence.

I back away from you abruptly. Slowly I bring one finger to my lips. I hold it there and I look at you. I walk closer, careful not to touch you, not to give my position away. Swiftly, I yank your head further backward thrusting my finger into your mouth. You moan and I can see the gulp in your throat. My fingers tighten over it as if to hold it there as I taste the blood on your tongue; my tongue smearing your blood over the roof of your mouth. Swirling to touch every tooth, every taste bud, I ravish your mouth and take what's left of your breath away. Struggling to maintain my senses, I relish the thought of us sampling your blood together. A growl escapes me, and I deepen the kiss. The tighter my grasp gets, I can feel your urge to speak. Still tightening, I can barely feel any air leaving your mouth at all. Yet just as quickly as I was there, I was gone again.

Moments pass as I reenter the dining room. You are moaning softly now, and I can see the shudders racking your body from the water that has chilled on your skin. Whimpers of frustration as you wonder where I'd gone and why I had chosen that moment to leave you. Suddenly you perk up...you can smell something.

"Vanilla?"

"DID I SAY YOU COULD SPEAK?"

"No, Mistress."

The aroma becomes stronger in the room. Again, you perk up, trying to determine my next move and wondering at the smell that drives you wild.

"Please, please..."

My palm connected with your face and your knees buckled. You would have collapsed had your arms not been firmly in place.

"Shhhh."

You recover and I can almost hear your thoughts as you wonder at the silence in the room. Standing there with a smile almost that of the Cheshire Cat, I watch you as you are trying to anticipate my next move. Inches above skin and so close to you that you can feel my breath at your neck, I move as if to kiss you. Then you felt the first drop. A faint burning sensation on your nipple as the wax met the wetness of your skin. A whimper escaped you, but your body craved more. You twist in the cuffs, straining to be closer, to move closer to where you imagined the candle to be.

The next drop fell onto your back and elicited another moan. The vanilla scent driving you insane as it mixes with the scent of your passion.

I tilt the candle further and watch as its wax rains down on your skin. Each drop causing you to move, writhe, and buckle against your restraints. You want to speak but know better. My arm is moving to order the droplets strategically over your shoulder, your breast, your back...even on your slightly tilted neck. Your moans are like music to my ears. I lean the candle closer to your body. Not close enough to cause any real fleshly damage, but close enough so that you feel more of the burning sensation and hear the sizzle as hot wax hits still wet skin.

You are panting now. The droplets have stopped coming. I have stopped moving. You can still smell the candle and the smoke from the still burning wick. But you do not know my next move. Your pussy is throbbing in anticipation, but your heart is pounding in fear of the unknown. Your head whips in every direction, straining to sense me.

Sharp nails against your flesh, coming at you in every direction, the feel of miniscule follicles of hair being ripped from you caused a whimper to escape as I claw the dried wax from your body. Arms moving in a circular motion, similar to that of a windmill, only with the speed of a box fan, piece by piece of wax are torn away. Tiny particles of pleasure and pain are dropping weakly away as if nothing. Your moans increase as the rhythm of my nails does not diminish.

"PLEASE, MISTRESS!"

The moment the last hiss slips from your tongue, my nails dig into your throat, my breath a low growl across your ear, and your toes strain to touch the floor. Fiercely gripping your throat, I could feel the fear pour off you as you hear the snarl that radiates from me. You fail at your attempt to inhale and I can feel the gulp try to erupt, the pulse throbbing against my fingers. I can taste your pleasure as my teeth dig into your shoulder.

"Shhhh." The sound rings with calmness, yet my patience wears thin at your disobedience. Effortlessly, I reach upward and unhook the chain that holds you bound. Turning you so that your back is firmly against my chest, your body slinks into me. You're trembling no longer from the wetness of your body, but from the chills of pleasure that overwhelm you.

I jerk you roughly backward, my tongue on your throat. Your life force drums furiously against the strain and I couldn't help but taste.

A growl escapes me as my lips open wide and prepare for me to bite down into your delicate flesh. Not gentle this time, but as an animal starved for too long. Not caring that the flesh is tender, not caring that blood is spilled, and not hearing the low cry that rolled from your lips. Small trails of blood formed from the spot where my teeth were buried, the fingers of my hand trailing one at a time. Not once lifting my teeth from your neck, I insert one blood-soaked finger into your mouth, swirling it over your tongue.

Holding you to me, with teeth in shoulder, one bloody finger thrust into your mouth, my other hand reaches around to the source of all your heat. My fingertips find your swollen bud, circling, until your body reacts, arcing upward and trying to pull away from the grip my teeth have on you. I watch the blood continue to flow. I sense your need. You are still blindfolded. You cannot anticipate my next movements, but your body is craving whatever that move may be.

Roughly, I thrust two fingers into your hot pussy. Fast, deep, and hard, causing your body to contract and fight to remain in one place. But the pleasure wants to tear your body in pieces. You can't escape the teeth in your neck. Your tongue craves the finger in your mouth. But your pussy is drawn to the fingers inciting tidal waves to form in your hips and back.

Sensory overload...the smell of your blood mixed with the scent of the vanilla candle. The pain of the teeth continuing to bite into your neck and the heat building at your core distracted you. There is no way you could have known or been prepared to go flying forward so suddenly.

Your head snapped forward as I shoved you away from me. It was hard enough to shake you from the melting pot of sensation and land you bent forward over the table directly in front. Palms hot, arms trembling to hold the weight of your upper body, weak from being suspended above your head and yet you refused to let your face connect with the surface. I smirk, realizing that you like being defiant.

I have given you only one order: silence, but you already know the unspoken rules. You like testing my patience. You like defying me, knowing the consequences. You are breathing hard, not from exertion, but from the excitement because you know what's coming and you brace yourself.

You feel me behind you as the pressure from the palm of my hand shoving downward smacks your cheek firmly against the surface of the cherry wood table. You can taste blood as your teeth tear into your lip and the slightest smile crosses your face. Hand still firmly planted at the base of your neck, I shove my fingers into you from behind. Three this time. You are dripping wet and they glide inside effortlessly, the tip of my thumb rimming your asshole as I thrust my fingers in and out of your pussy. Loving the low moans, I thrust deeper. Just as suddenly as I put them in, they came out. You jump as you feel warm wetness and sharp nails roam over your pussy lips. My fingers spread your juices from your clit to your ass...back and forth. Then suddenly I am gone. The sudden abandonment causing you to buckle and whimper in need, you moan soft, low, and long.

You feel my absence like a physical blow. You sense my presence but don't know quite where I am in the room. Should you risk it?

"Please."

And I am there.

You feel the straps hit your ass simultaneously and separately. Inexplicable, each sting has its own type of pain, yet it is all heavenly. I flick the whip across your ass, not wanting to rip flesh, but enough to warn you that disobedience will not continue to be tolerated. Your hips sway and I can see your juices flowing freely down your legs. I reach two fingers down to smear the wetness over your ass. I use my nails to embed your juice in your flesh, the mere touch sending waves of sensation over you and causing you to bite harder on your lip.

I flick the whip again, this time across your back and you immediately arch like a cat poised to attack. I alternate. Several steady flicks over your ass and a fast one over random parts of your body, and I enjoy this game of cat and mouse.

Your body is moving in rhythms now. You have gotten comfortable. Expecting the now familiar sting and pattern of the whip, you tense in anticipation. Hips moving in the tidal waves I love so much and yet I am not ready to satisfy that need just yet. I walk closer to you. Caressing the red marks on your ass left by the whip, hearing you whimper at the mix of pleasure and pain.

Giggles. You hear the unfamiliar sound as one drip from the melting ice cube hits your throbbing red ass cheek. You jerk upward reeling at the sound of an unfamiliar voice and shocked at the contrast in sensations. Cold on skin already burning making you want to scream out, but you know you can't.

Just as suddenly as you jerked upward, my palm is there to slam your face back against the table. Defiant, you still strain to guess the person's identity and position in the room. A mix of fear, curiosity, and elation consume you as you attempt to focus your senses. I chuckle as I can hear the thoughts in your brain...

Who is it? When did she enter? Why didn't I smell her? Hear her? What is she here for? When did she get the ice? Oh my God, it feels good!

Mmmmmm.

Flick! The whip hits your ass again. Still in the familiar pattern, but you are no longer sure of the next move in the game. Trembling now, emotions cascade through you. Flick...again with the whip, but you can hear no other sounds, can't distinguish exactly where the mystery woman is or what she will do.

Flick!

"Oh, my God!"

The tails of the whip land on your ass just as two ice cubes are placed in the center of your back. Droplets roll off your sides as contact with your skin begins to melt them instantly. Convulsing begins as the pattern of the whip accelerates and ice cubes begin touching random parts of your body. Your brain spins because you know I can't possibly be placing the ice cubes alone and even with a second set of hands, it was not possible.

A moan escapes as three fingers thrust inside your pussy from beneath you. The whipping continues... Shivers run through you as another sliver of ice is held against your breast. In and out, the fingers continuously delve into your pussy, ice on your back and breast, whip assaulting your ass cheeks and still more ice being placed at your lips. Then it registers: your body goes rigid with the knowledge that there are more people in the room!

The stranger is closer now...without warning, your right arm is yanked across the table away from your body. You could make out two hands, sharp nails, and soft skin. Nails that felt like razors from your shoulder to your wrists as the woman took authority of your arm. Beyond that, you are clueless as to the identity of the person who assisted me in holding you captive.

"Mistress!"

It was a word containing as much shock as it was a question and your left arm follows the first. Yanked firmly away from your body, by another set of hands, you have no choice but to be completely helpless against the table. More soft skin more nails, your rigid nipples getting even harder from the cold surface.

I laugh out loud now, because I know you are wondering how you missed the sound of people entering the room, wondering how long they'd been there. You are moaning louder now, and I know I need to step in before you wake the children.

"Sweet One, Shhhh!" It is a direct and abrupt order. You could hear the seriousness to my tone. Just as swiftly as I had given that one, I give the next one.

"Now!"

"Yes, Mistress."

It was hard to tell how many voices were in the room. You whimper in amazement as you realize every person in the room is here for one purpose. They're here to follow my orders, and those orders were to please you.

At that moment, you feel your legs forcefully widened. Held in place by hands that appeared out of nowhere, they shake with apprehension and excitement. It seems to you as if a thousand hands were roaming your body at once. Each arm was already held hostage, now each leg. Moans flooded your lips, you can't see, but you can feel. Pussy juices flowing freely now, so much you'd almost think you'd cum. The excitement only continued.

Fully taken hostage now, you squirm...not to free yourself, but in the effort to stem the burning and hunger within you. Someone grabs a fistful of your hair with one hand and holds your neck firmly planted to the table with the other. You try to focus, but a vanilla scent has been placed near your nose, and you can only assume the candle has been placed on the table in front of your face.

Each of the women holding your arms take turns raking their nails across the delicate skin, following quickly with their tongues as if to taste any blood that may appear there. Senses in an uproar, you struggle to focus, feel the different assaults on your body that has continued for hours now. Sharp pains cause your body to arch upward. Nails raking down your spine and ending in a curve along your belly was pure heaven.

Now convulsing legs are given the same treatment as fingers are replaced with a strap-on and a finger on your clit. Ferocity building, it's hard to focus now.

No longer are the attentions being paid to your body slow or rhythmic, but the pace increasing.

"More."

Whirlwind motion, you can't see, but can feel and your body shakes with the urgency. The person with the strap-on thrusts hard and fast into your pussy, juices making the sloshing noise you are so fucking wet. One finger is in your ass building the intensity, while the rest of your body is accosted by tooth and nail. Nostrils filled, pussy filled, your body is close to that ultimate release...

Someone leans in close to whisper, "Are you having fun?"

Slap! You hear the sound, and you flinch, but it takes you a moment to realize that it was not you who received it. Apparently, the rules apply to everyone in the room. Oddly though, the motions never stopped. Your body was still being accosted and you could feel the need to cum overwhelming you. Burning in your gut and just as the pleasure was reaching the apex...

"Stop."

"You can't cum yet, sweet one." It's whispered into your ear as if from some inanimate object. My voice is weightless. You couldn't tell if mine had been one of the pairs of hands that had been touching you.

Suddenly and effortlessly, your body is jerked upward. Blindfold forcefully removed, as your arms are held behind you. Your eyes are cloudy as you struggle to focus in the now bright room. Throat dry and still you want to speak as you notice five strange women in the room. All of them wearing collars and staring as if you are their very last meal.

Moans and whimpers escape as you realize there must be a sixth woman holding your chains because I am standing directly in front of you. You cannot move as your arms are chained directly behind you to a hook you never remembered seeing before this night. Slowly, your gaze meets mine, and you are mesmerized. I walk closer, letting my tongue roam over yours. My lips depart and you lean forward as if to keep them near.

Your attention is drawn to two of the women moving a reclining chair to the spot your body had just been in. They seem to be in uniform. All of them had raven black hair, long pointy nails, heeled black boots, and black leather collars that mimicked your own. You watch as the same two women lead me backward, away from you, to the chair. This chair was brown, seated low, with wide arm rests.

Seated in the chair, you moan as you watch one of the women kiss me, tongue dancing with mine, deeply, and wonder how my eyes never left yours. One by one, each of the women, including the one who had been previously out of view, walk to me, and all you can do was watch.

Watch as one stood behind me fisting my hair just enough for me to feel it, but not enough to tear my gaze away from yours. Watch as one begins to kiss the woman holding my hair. The kiss is one of lust and pure pleasure. Ravenous would be the only way to describe it, but the woman never breaks rhythm in the pulling of my hair.

More whimpers as a woman takes my breast in her mouth and you can see her tongue circling my areola. My nipples harden and you can see that I am enjoying the teasing, but my eyes never leave yours.

You break the stare as you realize two women are beside me on the floor in the sixty-nine position. Low murmurs of pleasure escaping as they stick their tongues deeply inside each other. You can see the pussy of the one on top, and she is so wet, it makes you lick your lips...alternating, biting and licking.

As if reading my mind, your gaze returns to mine, and you see as I prop each of my legs on the corresponding arm rest. You watch as the last remaining woman kneels before me and begins to lick my pussy. You can see her tongue darting around my clit. Sucking my pussy lips into her mouth one at a time, she makes popping noises as she enjoys her task.

Fingers now in her hair, you watch as I bury her face in my pussy. A moan escapes me as I watch the passion in your eyes and feel the hot tongue dipping deeply in and out of my pussy.

"Lick that pussy."

I smile as I see the moisture glistening on your legs. You are quivering and you are still not allowed to cum. Another rule you are firmly aware of.

Once again, concentration is broken as your eyes follow the sounds of the kisses and licks of the other women. I can see your mouth as it begins to pout for release. I stem the flow of my own moan as my pleasure is about to peak.

"Stop"

All movement in the room ceased.

"Are you ready to cum, sweet one?"

"Yes, Mistress."

As if following some script, the women take their places near the chair as one walks nearer to you to unchain you. Steps falter as you come closer, still not knowing what to expect. All your questions are soon answered as you are forced to your knees. Two women regain their respective positions at your arms and one woman holding your hair, forcing your face directly towards my pussy. One begins kissing me as your tongue swirls rhythmically over my clit.

I can feel your thoughts as you stop to wonder at the tasks assigned to the remaining two women. Almost as suddenly as you stop, a harsh pull to your hair reminds you not to forget what you are supposed to be doing. As quickly as you restart your task, your questions are again answered.

One woman takes her place behind you and the instant she rams into your pussy, you feel a ferocious grip on your neck. This propels your movements. You are so wet; it is pouring from you. You hear my moans, feel the grip on your neck tighten, feel the punishment your pussy is receiving, and you begin to shake. Nails rake into your hair and you struggle because you are prone, but your tongue never stops twirling, darting, in and out. You can only imagine the way I am kissing the woman and you begin to whimper.

My moans increase and you can feel my pussy tightening on your tongue as you thrust inside. You know I am about to cum, and it excites you.

As if on cue, the thrusting into your pussy quickens and the grip on your throat steals even the tiniest of breaths. The beat of your heart and the throbbing in your pussy could almost be music as you feel yourself about to explode....

Intent on your task, you can't see that every single woman is using a free hand to thrust inside their pussies. You can't see or feel their urgency coming on...and in unison...with one breath, we all cum...hard.

"Mmmmmm."

It was a simultaneous sound. It was pure pleasure. One by one, the women filed out of the room. Free from your restraints, you stand, and I pull you onto my lap. Before I could say anything, I hear your soft snores fill my ears....and the morning light found us that way.

Warm Velvet

Sandra Hamlin

Well I won't pretend that this is one of those love at first sight, fairy tale kind of stories. There were never any starry eyes or dream come true soulmate expectations. I mean, I wasn't looking for a soulmate—just a soul to date.

See, I had been at peace with my piece since having a divorce two years earlier from an abusive butch. I gave up a beautiful house on half an acre, and everything I put into it, in exchange for my life and my sanity. Backed that proverbial U-Haul truck up over my rose-colored glasses and moved into a sprawling one-bedroom apartment in a Jersey suburb.

Once I got my bearings, there was a perpetual smorgasbord of women in New Jersey. And with the help of the internet, I found myself smack dab in the midst of a lesbian extravaganza of sexual debauchery.

But there was one woman in particular—all metrosexual male energy—who was a safe distance away in Delaware. Though handsome in a latte hued Ellen DeGeneres way, she wasn't really my type. I sent a note to say hello and compliment her on how well her profile was written and wished her luck on her journey in finding "the one." After all, my dating plate was full. So, naturally she wrote back, and we exchanged phone numbers.

Initially, we didn't jibe at all. Shades of oil and vinegar. After the second phone conversation in which we argued about things we actually agreed on (don't ask) we adamantly vowed to cut bait and delete contact info. So, when she called the next day with a cleverly disguised apology, I told her this Aries/Capricorn conversion was clearly a no go. There would be no meshing of hearts or body parts.

Undaunted, she asked me what my moon sign was. For those of you who are not into astrology, your moon sign represents who you are deep inside once you let folks in. Not only was her moon in Gemini to my Aries moon, but she knew the zodiac signs of scores of celebrities, writers and musicians as I did. This warm fuzzy feeling of intrigue and appreciation washed over me. I thought, ok, she's as crazy as I am. This could work.

Now, it hasn't always been easy. On the surface we are an eccentric mix of ebb and flow. She is antique teacups, stacks of books and eclectic jazz. Her style of dress is perfectly polished conservative. She is penny pinching practical and prefers documentary, biographical and spiritual films. I am more of an all-inclusive, impulsive mixture of bohemian creativity. Like a classic rock and old school rap collaboration. I am Brunswick stew and foreign beers (in a glass please). I like spy thrillers, shoot 'em ups and comedies. My preferred style of dress is loose and artsy.

I think she must have conjured my love from the very start. Yet she always tells me that I am magic. Imagine if you will, what it might feel like to be ensconced in warm velvet. Cozy. Content. Our first date was a weekend of thunderstorms, music and slow dancing in the moonlight. I remember the song, "For the Love I Give to You" by the Delfonics came on. I said oh, I LOVE this song! Well she and her swag got up, turned to me and extended her hand...

Twelve years later we still dance. In the kitchen, in the sunroom—sometimes when I enter a room her face lights up, she extends her hand, and we will dance to something as simple as a TV commercial. Then when she says, "Come on, honey. Let's snuggle up," I get that same warm fuzzy feeling. Whether we're sipping tea or watching a comedy...

Warm velvet.

Cadence

Louise Lamar

"Come on. I want to show you something."

I wasn't sure if I wanted to follow her after our last fiasco. Stacy and I had only been dating for six months although our connection made it seem that we had known each other for years. I felt an odd connection like we were meant to be, like she was a gift to me. I didn't think...no I knew I had never met anyone who felt like a gift to me. Someone or something in the universe had felt I deserved this special kind of love. You know, the kind of love when a person walks into a room and sparkles while everything else fades away.

She had already taken me on a tour of her life. We went to her close friends' homes, and I met her sister. But, the most amazing thing was when she took me to her hometown. I didn't expect the privilege of visiting her youth vicariously through her memories and meeting her Nana.

I remember that was the first time she wanted to take me somewhere.

"I want to show you something, but you have to ride with me."

I remember looking at her because at that time we had only known each other for a month. What, is she crazy? She thinks that I am gonna ride with her in her car so she can take me somewhere and kidnap or kill me? Hell, no.

I answered cautiously, "I'll follow you in my car. Where to?"

"I want to show you where I grew up. My Nana's and grandmother's houses. You won't let me kidnap you?" Her sensuous smile was a bit wicked, which intrigued and frightened me all at once.

I giggled, maybe more from discomfort than humor, but I retorted, "I'll still drive myself." I couldn't believe it, I was going. My curiosity might just kill the proverbial cat.

We drove for about a half hour to an hour. I kept thinking, where the hell is she taking me. She really is on some kill-a-girl-out-in-the-country bullshit. And, here I am, a damn fool, following her. I heard my mother's voice in my head, "Don't go to people's houses and did you give a number or address to someone so we can find you?" Here I am going into a small town that looks like somebody's backwoods.

Finally, we pulled into this little driveway in front of a quaint house that looked like it was made of gingerbread devoid of the icing and gumdrops. The front door was a little crooked but as we approached an old woman in a wheelchair rolled out of the front door.

"Hey, you made it." The woman was waving her white handkerchief frantically as if we were across a field and not just thirty feet away.

I looked at Stacy as she quickly moved up the walkway and hugged the little woman in the chair. "This here is my Nana, Genie Mae."

I bent down and softly placed my hand in hers. Just then she firmly grabbed my hand and shook it aggressively saying, "I'm old but strong."

"Yes ma'am, yes you are," I giggled.

"NaNa, remember I can drive you..." Stacy turned NaNa and pushed her into the house. I walked slowly up the walkway looking at all of the beautiful veggies planted on both sides. Nana clearly planted edibles everywhere on her property. Hmmm. I didn't know brussels sprouts grew on a stalk.

"Are you comin', or what?" she said looking back over her shoulder at me.

That smile...I knew at that moment that I loved her. Her half devious smile lulled me in love.

That beautifully devious smile lulled me right to her old bedroom in her Nana's house after she had gone to her doctor's appointment. As Nana's special transportation picked her up, we rushed to the bedroom like two little girls racing to the sandbox. Once in the bedroom, Stacy convinced me to use a strap-on for the first time, ever. She talked all sorts of dirty to me.

"Smack it like it's yours. Go deep, you're a beast. Hurt me, big daddy," she said playfully as she bit my earlobe.

I had never had anyone entice me this way and whoa it got my juices flowing on blast. I did my very best to follow her orders and oh it was wonderful, the sounds, smells, flavors—oh, I was wrapped in her magic. It was a whirl of body parts, laughs, giggles, exhalations and rhythms. I was so into this woman that her smacking me in my face, yelling "get up," was never heard. I continued my indulgence of her until I heard a car door slam. I sat up and looked at her. All she could say was, "Yeah, Nana is back."

OMG, the flood of fear that hit me. Of all the stories Stacy told me about her Nana, I remember two things, mostly that many of them involved her Nana pointing a gun at some indiscriminate stranger or some problematic family member. And the other is that she didn't like any doors closed in her house unless she closed them. All the rooms had curtains as doors, including the bathroom to emphasize her desire. At this point I was neither family nor stranger, but it didn't matter.

Finally, I was fully dressed but as I looked in the mirror the pink dildo was still firmly strapped on after some moments of tugging.

"Stacy," I turned to ask for help, but she was gone. I stepped into the hallway, "Stacy?" I called again toward the small kitchen. Her damn ass had evacuated the premises, leaving me standing in the hallway with a pink erect dildo through my unzipped jeans.

I heard Nana rolling her way up the wooden ramp. I quickly tucked pinky into my pants. I looked down, and the bulge was fantastic and huge. I ran into the living room, jumped over the ottoman and landed in the cozy chair, grabbed the remote, turned to the Price is Right and opened a magazine to place in my lap.

OMG. I inhaled deeply, and the front door swung open.

"You know I don't like doors shut in my house," she said in a bitter tone that, I swear, almost made me poop my pants.

When I answered, my voice was shaking, "No, ma'am. I wasn't aware."

"You know I don't like doors shut in my house," she chastisingly reiterated.

"Yes, ma'am," I responded hoping that this was the correct answer to stop her sinister scrutiny that felt like I was in a Hitchcock movie, expecting Nana to stand and come at me with an axe. And still, Stacy was nowhere to be found. She had truly run like a scared little bitch.

Nana rolled past me barely missing my toes with her wheelchair. "You want something to eat?"

I pointed my feet and snatched them back against the chair I was sitting in, "Yes, ma'am."

"You like pinto beans and beets?"

"Yes, ma'am." I didn't know what else to answer. Pinto beans and beets as a last meal. Ok. After all, we were the only two in the house and I felt it was better for me to just be agreeable. It was safer...no, I was safer saying yes.

"Nana, you're back." Stacy entered through the kitchen door carrying a bucket. "I poured the soapy water in your garden."

Nana, without looking up, said, "I told her I don't like my doors closed."

Stacy shifted nervously from leg to leg. "Yeah, I told her. I poured it on the cabbage."

I looked over my eye-glasses at Stacy from the living room. What a punk, I thought. Damn, she ran outside and then came back in with a prop. She left me alone to suffer the barrage of silent accusations enveloped in Nana's insistence.

Standing next to her Nana at the kitchen sink, Stacy side-eyed me and slightly smiled and oh all I could do was smile and giggle. Her punk-ass just keeps stealing my heart. But still, I wasn't too sure about going places with her. She always led us into some oddly dangerous adventure.

Just as now I had no idea why I am standing here looking at a house in the distance.

"Are you coming, or what?" she said with a giggle as she peered back at me over her shoulder.

I hadn't noticed that I was just standing at the edge of the overgrown grassy path watching her sinuous figure rhythmically hacking away with a machete at the overgrowth.

Stacy was beautiful.

"Yes, I am coming." I hiked up my floral-printed skirt and tied it in knots just above my knee to keep it from snagging on the ragged grass and occasional spiky stem. I caught her eyeing my soft legs before she returned her attention to clearing our path towards the boarded-up home. After a few exhaustive hacks at a honeysuckle bush, releasing sweet summertime scent, that had grown across the podiums up to the doorway, we could clearly see the remains of a red door. She pried off the foreclosure sign. She turned towards me and with a deep bow at her waist gesturing toward the house with her left hand she said, "Voila, my lady. This is it."

"Ok, it's a house. Why are we fighting nature to get to a house?" I began to fan the small gnats that had emerged from the honeysuckle. She extended her hand and pulled me to her on the porch. My body warmed against hers as she balanced me with her arm around my waist.

"Well, I bought it. It's mine." She looked at me intensely.

I turned my attention away a little, feeling a tad overwhelmed by the closeness.

"And well, it's yours...if you will live with me."

I pulled away a little. "What do you mean mine and living together?"

She dropped her arm and turned on her heels. "You know you feel it. I feel it...this energy, this thing between us. You know there will be no one else." She stood at the end of the porch staring at me. "You are beautiful."

"Something is wrong with your eyes," I joked. I knew I looked a mess. I began untying the knots in my skirt and readjusting my locks. I brushed off the sticky grass balls that lined the bottom of my skirt. "Can we look inside?" I inquired, needing to change the subject.

"Yes, the grand tour begins." She removed the key from her pocket and nudged open the door.

We entered the foyer.

"Imagine," she stepped center stage and spread her fingers wide above her, "a crystal chandelier perfectly centered above the marble floors." She danced me back and forth across the floor as my eyes flashed at the notion of people and parties. I smiled as I listened to the clickety-clack of my heeled sandals on the marble floor.

"Next level." Stacy grabbed me around my waist and ushered me upstairs to the master bedroom. We sauntered through the huge airy room to the master bathroom.

"Is that a lake?" I asked as she helped me step into the tub to sit on the edge and look out the window. The lake was mercury with a backdrop of wooded mountains beyond the flowering trees. I noticed in my periphery that Stacy's eyes were fixed on me, reveling in my joy of the view.

"You will see this every time you take a bath after a long day at work. We could sit here in an evening bubble bath, sipping wine, and watching the sunset."

I stood up. "See, you think you're slick." I stepped out of the tub and rushed back to the stairwell.

"No wait...wait," she was beside me with her hand on my elbow. "I just know...I am sure that I want you." Not taking her eyes from mine, she slowly slid her hands to my waist.

"I know...I know you believe...At least, I feel that I know you. You are earnest in your love and that is why I love you. I mean..." I panicked. I had gone too far. I had never said "I love you" to her. I turned and walked down the stairs.

"What's over here?" I redirected my thoughts towards another room.

"This is the kitchen," she said as she stepped in. "See how spacious it is." We stood in front of the French double doors that she opened to a walking garden that needed care. She remembered that I loved mountains, lakes, baths at sunset and the garden.

"This will be our breakfast nook." I looked over at her. I knew that she knew I would stay. That this would be our home. She knew that there would be no others.

"We will have a wonderful breakfast every day." She smiled.

Stepping onto the deck, we stood there looking at each other, and then at the garden. She stood behind me as she hugged me, nuzzling the back of my head with the tip of her nose. I leaned back into her, feeling the cadence of her breathing with mine as I held the circle of her arms to me.

This is my life. I looked at the beautiful scene and felt safe and knew this was right. This is my home. With Stacy is my home.

Holding hands, we rounded the porch to the west side of the house. She pulled me close to her with her hand on the round of my hip. We lowered onto the pollen covered love-seat swing. I leaned into her, looked up at her bourbon brown eyes and whispered, "I want to sit here on our tenth anniversary and watch the sunset just as we are doing right now."

And, we rocked to the sunset.

Taste

Moisterous

Close your eyes 'cause for you I have an orgasmic surprise and it's found right between those sexy, thick thighs.

Now imagine me pushing you against the wall while I whisper in your ear and my name you gently call.

As I bite the side of your neck and pull your hair, you look into my eyes without a care, 'cause when you are with me I will take you there.

Beyond your deepest fantasy, that's where you will find me.

Making my way from your neck to your waist, girl, you got me for only one night, and we got no time to waste,

So don't be scared, take a deep breath and let me dive in to taste.

I'm diving into your glorious ocean; damn, this shit is the love potion.

They say pineapples do the trick, but you think you're slick 'cause you know this shit is the lick.

The taste of you is like being high for the first time; you say this your first time but I think you're lying,

'Cause from down here we're flying and oh shit you're crying, maybe you ain't lying.

I move you from the wall and throw you on the bed and proceed to give you more head,

Don't try to shut those legs.

Go ahead and scream, it's okay; that's how I know I am hitting that spot the right way.

Don't be shy to tell me what you crave; tonight I am your sex slave.

So please melt in my mouth and take me into your Deep South,

'Cause the taste of you is what I am all about!

Bound.

L.M. Bennett

"Do you trust me?"

"I don't have much of a choice at the moment," I say, as she tugs on the rope. It pulls a loop around my left thigh. Not tight or bruising, but just enough pressure to remind me it's there.

I'm wearing nothing but ropes and knots by design. At her hand. She stands above me surveying her work, and occasionally her gaze lingers in places that pull me tighter than the rope.

Trust, I'd rather pull her in deeper to me. Maybe it's a good thing my hands are tied at the moment.

The modesty pad tucked between thick thighs doesn't offer much to hide other than my mound. I squeeze them together so she can't see how much this is getting to me.

If she flips me over, I'll have to explain some things I'd rather not. Might embarrass myself and lean into her touch. Moan if she strokes long fingers down my backside. Bite my lip with a slap.

My laugh is equal parts embarrassment and frustration.

"You're enjoying this too much," she says, tying a knot between my ankles. My toe brushes against the silk sheet underneath.

"Why don't you come see how much?" Even the words feel breathless, chest heaving against the ropes. The press of the fibers against my nipples is almost too much.

She's being respectful, professional, but her eyes linger between my legs.

"Be a good girl." She traces a whisper across my ankles with the back of her hand.

I'm all tied up, but she's the one who looks pinned down. "Never."

The set of the music video is electric, a mishmash of silk, neon lights, leather and spikes. Exotic flowers. The leather couches are inviting, and you can almost feel their embrace with every caress. There's a wooden table with an ass-print carved in. Bright spotlights dance around us like stars in a night sky, highlighting the beauty and power of the woman beside me. There are scantily clad extras as far as the eye can see. Big body gals, I heard in a song once. Curves spilling like milk out of bustiers and garter belts. Skin shiny and smooth, from butterscotch to dark chocolate.

My heart races when she steps closer. Her fingers brush against mine and I feel a rush of electricity shoot through my veins like a comet blazing a trail across the universe. She leans in close enough for me to smell the sweet honey on her lips. My hands reach out instinctively for her waist but find themselves restrained by ropes instead. We linger there for a moment before she pulls away, leaving me bewitched and yearning for more.

The director of the music video claps his hands, and she immediately steps away from me, her eyes lingering on my bare form. I eye her right back.

A promise for later. Much later, without the cameras and the PAs trying to look uninterested.

As the director sets up for the shot, I take a deep breath and close my eyes. The studio is alive with activity: crew members adjusting lights, producers discussing camera angles. Through it all, her gaze burns hot on my flesh. Though I am in nothing but ropes and knots, I feel more powerful than ever before.

The cameras roll as a purple spotlight shines directly on me. I can feel the energy radiating through me as I writhe to the rhythmic pulse of the song playing over the set. Words I probably wrote while high set to some producer's slowed down beat.

My eyes blink open, and the purple light reflects off my skin as I look directly into the camera. For a moment, it feels like I'm looking right into her eyes, and I imagine her standing there watching me as if nothing else matters in that moment. No director. No crew. Just us.

"Just like that," the director says, pacing behind the cameraman. "Beautiful."

I imagine myself as a puppet pulled by an invisible force—the string of emotion that connects us both—and it moves through me like waves crashing against the shoreline. Every move feels natural—a part of something larger than myself.

I can almost hear her heart beating faster as she takes in my bound body and reads what I'm not saying out loud; I'm surrendering myself completely to her.

The fantasy deepens. I imagine her tugging my hair back, reaching down and kissing me roughly. Firm hand gently gripping my throat. Arousal shoots through me at the thought of her taking control, and I can't help but let out a soft moan. The inside of my thighs is slippery wet.

There's nothing I want more in this moment than for her to bury her bald head between my thighs to taste the slickness. The throbbing is unbearable.

It's taking everything in me to keep from humping the sheet below. I mouth the words to the song, imagining myself singing to her and only her.

No one else notices, or maybe they do, but in that moment, it feels like we're the only two people in the world.

In my mind's eye, her hands move to the knots at my wrists. I'm so aroused that I can barely keep my eyes open as she frees me from the rope.

My breathing is ragged and heavy in anticipation of what's coming next. I feel her fingertips skim over my skin as she moves up and down my body, exploring every inch with a soft touch, setting little fires wherever she goes.

Her lips find mine and we both moan into each other's mouths hungrily. My body feels alive and yearning for something more. She takes one of my wrists in hers, still gripping tightly to me, as if to remind me who's in control here.

With trembling hands she cups my chin and brings her mouth down between my legs, tasting all the wetness there as if it were a fine wine she'd patiently waited to savor for years now.

I'm damn near eye-fucking the camera at this point. They're half-mast while I sing along, rolling on the floor. My back arches off the ground. The camera angles low to eye-level, lest everyone watching this video get an eyeful of chocolate nipples, still with cool air and my own arousal.

My eyes find hers again. She's got one muscular arm folded around her, with the other hand at her mouth. Tongue darting out to taste her thumb.

While the fantasy her is bold and unyielding as she devours me, the real her looks away. Then, slowly back. Head to toe.

Good.

The intensity radiates between us.

I close my eyes and imagine her looking up from my spread thighs. I can almost feel every slick inch of her tongue against me, and it's making me even more desperate for her. If it wasn't for the ropes binding me tight, I could probably crawl across the room to get to her, look up at her from between her strong thighs, and make this fantasy real.

I gasp in anticipation as she licks her tongue up the inside of my thigh, teasing ever so lightly with each stroke. Soon, she's kissing my clit, pulling, rolling, sucking. Each lick punctuated by a thrust of her fingers inside. My heart pounds in my chest as her tongue circles around my innermost parts; if this was real, I'd barely be able to contain myself at this point.

To heighten the experience further, she takes the rope still tied around my wrists and wraps it tightly between my legs like a vice grip on an orgasmic journey. All I can do is clutch helplessly at my own thighs and moan. The sensation is overwhelming as the rope rubs against me in just the right places with each pulse of heat that radiates through me.

As if on cue, our movements become faster and more intense with each passing second and soon enough my cries overtake the melody coming out of speakers behind us—the only thing keeping me grounded in reality amidst such reckless abandon for pleasure.

The rope is the final wave that crashes over me, leaving me completely enveloped in a sea of pleasure. I can feel every ripple of my orgasm as it surges through me, surprising me with its intensity. Its realness. Just as real as if she had been inside me, pulling the climax from me with her fingers and mouth.

And then it's over, and I'm lying there spent from my orgasm, still clinging to the rope that helped bring me such pleasure. I look up and find her on the other side of the room, dark eyes glinting. She looks amused.

The director calls cut.

My eyes close and I take a deep breath, feeling like I've just been brought back to earth from an amazing high. There's still a few moments of silence in the room before she finally steps forward. She reaches for the ropes around my wrists and begins untying them slowly, her hands gentle against my skin. She frees my legs and ankles in turn.

My body sings with relief from the tension of the pulling rope.

Once free, she reaches for a floral pink kimono coverup hanging nearby and slips it over my shoulders so that I'm no longer exposed; as if this simple garment could contain all the fire I made with her in my head. The cool whisper of silk against my thighs is a reminder.

Finally, she looks up at me with a smirk and speaks the words that I'd been hoping to hear ever since I first saw her: "Let's do it again. For real. No cameras."

I swallow, still feeling slow and buzzed with the warmth of pleasure coursing through my veins. My muscles give off a pleasant ache. And as I stand there in awe of this woman who has captured my imagination, only one word comes to mind.

"Yes."

Anticipation

Literary Stud

Early morning sunbeams pushed through the small slit in the drapes and across the mess of sheets and pillows on the plush bed. The television ran through a loop of hotel amenities, ways of ordering room service, and the current premium movie selections. Rayne dropped toiletries and a bag of dirty laundry in her suitcase. After a week away from home, she'd seen every movie worthy of wasting time on and a few that weren't. The writer's conference fell on the most romantic holiday of the year and originally, she planned for her wife, Thea, to accompany her for a couple's getaway. But at the last moment, Thea had a work crisis and couldn't make the trip. Instead of seeing New York City sights together, Rayne hid a gift in the house and had roses delivered with every intention of celebrating as soon as she stepped foot in the house. On Valentine's Day, they settled for a champagne toast and virtual lovemaking via video chat.

The alert of an incoming text message pierced through the rambling television and her horny thoughts. Rayne snatched the phone from the bed, expecting a message from Thea only to be disappointed by her subscription for the word of the day. Any other morning, she'd excitedly open the message, eager to learn an unknown word. Today she tossed the phone back on the bed in disgust and continued packing. She had a plane to catch. Rayne ached to feel Thea's skin against her own, to hear her name moaned while they engaged in rapturous delight and video chat left her more frustrated than before. Suffice to say, her impatience compounded with each passing hour but kept it in check mainly because of a promise. Thea took pity on her childish pout and promised Rayne her favorite position, making her even more eager to go home.

The last day of the conference had a social agenda of alcoholic mixers and Rayne had her fill of intoxicated wordsmiths. She changed her flight to leave a day early to surprise Thea. Rayne hummed through checking her bag at airport security, even smiling at fussy toddlers giving her the evil eye. The nearly four-hour flight breezed by as she daydreamed about her wife's kissable neck and delicious curves. She waited at the baggage claim with a wide smile and her heart pounded as the rideshare car sped toward home. Rayne locked the door and left her luggage in the foyer to follow the noises coming from the kitchen. Thea stood with her back to the entrance, cream slacks with red pinstripes hugged her hips and outlined the plump derriere Rayne loved to fondle. She flipped her curly hair across her shoulder, tilting her head ever so slightly and revealing the curve of her neck. Rayne closed the distance between them and placed a soft kiss on the bare skin.

Thea started. "Rayne, what are you doing here?"

"I left early." She spun Thea, pushing her against the island for a kiss. Willing lips kissed back as Thea leaned into Rayne, clutching at the strong arms, holding her tight. Fingers deftly unbuttoned her slacks and pushed them down to pool around her heels.

"Wait, Rayne," she muttered against her lips. "Not right now."

"What do you mean, not right now?"

"My book club meets this afternoon. They'll be here any minute." Thea pushed Rayne back some. "Now, I wish they weren't."

"Me too." Rayne trailed kisses up to her ears. "Why today?"

"Hmm? I can't think when you do that." Thea pushed against her again. "Because you weren't supposed to be home until tomorrow. I volunteered the house at the last minute. I wouldn't have if I'd known you'd be home early."

She smiled sheepishly. "I wanted to surprise you."

"You definitely did that." Thea caressed Rayne's ears, eyes focused on her soft lips. "I missed you."

"I missed you too, baby." Rayne kissed her again, slipping a hand between her thighs. Instinctively, Thea sidestepped to accept Rayne's persistent fingers. Her knuckles grazed the edge of lacy panties as the doorbell announced visitors. "Shit."

"A few more seconds and I don't think you would've stopped." Thea pulled her slacks up and straightened her clothes.

"I hadn't planned on it."

"It will be over in about three hours."

"Three hours?" Rayne sulked. "What are you reading? War and Peace?"

"Stop being so dramatic." Thea shook her head and rushed to the front door.

Rayne waited impatiently through the exclamations filled with comments on each other's attire and the beautiful decorations around the house. When Thea returned, she laughed at the frown plastered on Rayne's features and gave her a quick peck. Rayne didn't let go, deepening the glancing peck into a soul-stirring kiss. Her hands traveled down to Thea's ass, crushing their bodies together. Laughter erupted from the living room, breaking the moment and with considerable effort, Thea pulled away.

"Whew, ok. We obviously need to keep some space between us," she said.

"This sucks. What am I supposed to do for three hours?"

"You could stay and contribute to the group."

Rayne shook her head. "Nah, that's okay."

Thea laughed. "Okay. How about the driving range? You never have time to go."

She shrugged. "I guess, but I don't know how I'll focus."

"You aren't the only one disappointed." She leaned forward and gave Rayne a chaste kiss on the cheek. "And I have a promise to keep."

"I'll be back in two hours and forty-five minutes."

THWACK!

The dimpled golf ball sailed high in the air, arcing downward and landing beside the metal sign announcing one hundred and seventy-five yards. Rayne checked her watch again. Only twenty-three minutes. The drive to the range, paying for a bucket of balls, and scoring an empty spot killed about an hour of time. Twenty-four minutes and half the bucket already rested in various places around the driving range. Rayne looked down the line of golfers, hacking away their worries. She stood between a golf instructor with a novice pupil and a husky, sweating man dressed in the latest golf fashions, complete with a very expensive set of clubs. Unlike other enthusiasts, Rayne considered golf a leisure sport, a relaxing but intimidating gift from Scotland. A pleasurable battle between golfer and a little ball repeated throughout eighteen holes, surrounded by rolling hills, crystal blue lakes, and sometimes magnificent, towering, green trees.

Thea understood Rayne's obsession with golf, even though she had no interest in playing at all. They met at a charity event when her friend Landon invited her to play in a foursome at the last minute. The proceeds benefited domestic violence survivors and Thea headed the planning committee. Rayne stood in line for ten minutes before reaching the check-in table. Thea looked up from the clipboard and Rayne's gaze locked with sensual, brown eyes and a dazzling smile against a deep, melanated complexion. Thea gave Rayne an appreciative once over before asking her name. Landon elbowed her in the ribs, giving her a wink and a nod toward Thea as they walked away. They ran into Thea again while she drove a refreshment cart around the golf course, passing out bottles of water. Rayne and Landon waited with their foursome for the group ahead of them to tee off on the ninth hole. Thea handed them each a cold bottle with a double entendre about endurance and a pointed look at Rayne. Even though she thought the flirting happened to coincide with persuading potential donors, Rayne followed Landon's advice, rolled the dice, and approached Thea at the awards ceremony immediately after the tournament. By the end of the conversation, they exchanged numbers and had a coffee date.

But no matter how much crackling chemistry surrounded them, six months passed before they became intimate. A shiver ran through Rayne remembering the heights they climbed that night and most of the next day. Even now, as a married couple, their ardor remained an important aspect of their lives. Any other day, Rayne relished the opportunity to indulge in the expensive hobby but now she'd rather be in a compromising position, feasting on Thea. Gripping the five iron, she positioned her body for the slingshot swing and Thea's svelte form strutted around her imagination. The wanton bounce of her buxom breasts whenever she rode Rayne's fingers. She tried to shake the wanton images from her head but like the hook of a hit song, it stuck around. With a hard grunt, she struck the inoffensive ball with resounding force.

THWACK!

The ball veered to the right, drawing a conceited smirk from Mr. Husky. Rayne gave the man a salute, switched to a driver, and forced herself to focus. She hit a few balls off the tee, channeling every bit of impatience into each swing. The hours spent with a swing coach proved to be money and time well spent, even if Landon teased her about it. In the middle of the next swing, her cell phone vibrated. Thea.

"Hey, baby." Rayne stepped away.

"I love the way you say that," Thea murmured.

"I'll say it as many times as you like."

"Hmm. Are you almost done?"

"I can drop this at any moment," she replied, tugging her glove off. "I'm waiting on you."

"We're wrapping up early. If you leave now, they should be gone by the time you get home," Thea said. "Then we can finally celebrate Valentine's Day."

"I'm on my way." Rayne dropped the bucket next to Mr. Husky with a grin before trotting off with her golf bag.

Thea returned to the living room as the book club president announced the next selection on the list. They all thanked Thea for the hospitality and complimented her organization skills. Thea accepted with a smile, inwardly urging them to hurry up and leave. She checked the time. If she knew her wife, Rayne was pushing the speed limits to get home. While most of the women departed immediately, a few stayed behind to help straighten up. Thea assured them she could manage the mess, but one, an older lesbian named Esther, insisted and asked about the trash bags. Her skin tingled knowing when she arrived, the pent-up sexual frustration would last the rest of the day and possibly the night. Thea's attraction to Rayne hadn't lessened since the day they met at the golf tournament. Her smooth demeanor and full sensual lips, and not to mention the unmistakable deep timbre of Rayne's voice tugged at Thea's loins. Buried in the flirty and suggestive conversation, Rayne's intellect and view of the world intrigued her, holding her attention like no other stud had. Although Thea loved sex, she practiced restraint in her choice of partners. But the more time they spent together, she imagined what Rayne's sex would be like. She kept her hands to herself and had a few solo pleasurable moments fantasizing about Rayne and her smooth voice. As she remembered it, worth the wait.

Thea passed through the hallway leading to the kitchen as Rayne opened the front door. She paused long enough to bestow a come-hither look before slipping through the archway. Rayne closed the door and followed, catching Thea around the waist before spinning her around. Thea melted into Rayne, grabbing her shirt to get closer for a kiss. A soft moan escaped as their lips met. Thea slipped her arms around Rayne's neck, matching the fire threatening to consume her. She forgot about the cleaning straggler in the living room and allowed Rayne to back her against the marble island.

"I need to taste you," Rayne murmured, reaching down to lift Thea up.

"I think that's my cue to leave," Esther said with a hint of amusement.

They broke apart, awkwardly smiling at Esther who joked about the last time she was on a countertop. Rayne waited at the bottom of the stairs while Thea escorted Esther to the door. She returned with a sultry expression, unbuttoning her blouse to reveal a lacy, black bra. Rayne licked her lips and reached out for Thea's hand. Every few steps they kissed and discarded a piece of clothing until they reached the bed, naked and panting. Rayne sat Thea down on the bed to kneel in front of her and filled her hands with ample breasts before sliding her cheeks across each erect nipple. She continued a familiar path down her stomach, in pursuit of sustenance only Thea could give. Thea laid back on the bed, her hands grasping at Rayne's hair, anxiously pulling her closer. But as Rayne's chin grazed her swollen clit, Thea's legs tensed, and she pushed at her forehead.

"Rayne, the doorbell."

"Huh?"

"The doorbell," she repeated.

"Not happening, baby. Whoever it is, will have to come back another time."

"It could be important." She tried to scoot backwards on the bed.

Rayne held tight. "This is important."

"Go and see who it is," Thea replied, tone firm.

Rayne stood and grabbed the robe off the chaise. She stomped downstairs, checked the peephole, and shook her head. Another interruption. Friends since elementary school, Ali always seemed to pop up at the most inopportune moments. She opened the door. "What do you want, Ali?"

"Damn, I thought you'd never open the door."

"What do you want? I'm busy right now."

"Bruh, my car stopped up the street. I tried to call, but you didn't answer." Ali walked toward the kitchen. "You got anything to drink? I'm thirstier than a muthafucka."

"I told you I'm busy."

"Rayne?" Thea called from the top of the stairs. "Is everything okay?"

"Yeah. It's Ali. She was just leaving," Rayne answered, looking up at her. She found it. The black, silk robe she hid for Valentine's Day cascaded around Thea's voluptuous curves. She walked halfway up the stairs.

"You found it."

"I did. I love it."

"You could've waited until I gave it to you."

"I was missing you when I found it," she admitted.

"Come on, bruh," Ali piped up. "My car won't start."

"Her car won't start?" Thea asked.

"How're you doing, Miss Thea?"

"Fine, Ali." Thea backed up from view. "Are you going to help her?"

"I wasn't planning on it."

"Rayne."

"Baby."

"The quicker you go, the quicker you can get back. I'm not going anywhere."

Accepting defeat, Rayne stomped past Thea to change. "You owe me."

Thea followed. "She's your friend."

"She's blocking," she replied, pulling up her pants.

"You're ridiculous. Her car didn't break down to keep you from getting some."

"I wouldn't put it past Ali." Rayne crushed Thea to her for a kiss and headed back downstairs before Ali helped herself to food in the fridge.

"Say, bruh, did I interrupt something?" Ali asked as Rayne locked the door.

Rayne returned two hours later, with a thin layer of grease coating her hands and forearms. Ali possessed a fetish for cash cars with sketchy engines but had no clue about automotive repair. All of Rayne's experience came from her college years of keeping her own jalopy moving, often with duct tape and a prayer. Be that as it may, even her expertise had limitations. After toiling for an hour, Rayne paid for a tow truck. The setting sun pushed dusky beams through the bedroom drapes, falling across the bed and a sleeping Thea. Hugging the pillow, she lay on her stomach, the hem of the robe inching up and giving Rayne an eyeful of bare ass. She rushed to strip out of the filthy clothes for a shower. When she emerged a short time later, the bed was empty, and she heard voices downstairs. Rayne grabbed a robe and ran into Thea on the landing.

"Rayne! You scared me," Thea exclaimed. "What's wrong with you?"

"I thought someone was here again." Rayne's eyes fixed on her heaving breasts.

"No, I left my cell phone downstairs," she explained. "A book club member called about a lost earring."

"Oh." The robe shifted, unveiling more skin. "Did she leave one?"

"I told her I'd look for it." Thea narrowed her eyes. "Why are you looking at me like that?"

"Huh? Looking at you like what?" Rayne reached out for the sash, causing the robe to fall open, exposing her exquisite form.

"Very intensely."

She brushed her knuckles across the silky skin of her breasts. "I'm not in the mood for more interruptions."

"Okay." Thea gave Rayne a coy smirk as she walked past, her heated flesh tingling, remembering all too well what happened when Rayne reached her breaking point.

At the bed, Rayne kissed Thea, pushing the robe from her shoulders. Thea returned the favor by removing Rayne's robe, moaning when their bare skin finally touched. Thea felt the aggression flowing from Rayne, the frustration threatened to consume them both. Rayne broke the kiss, trailing her lips down the curve of Thea's neck and reaching a stealthy hand between her moist thighs.

"Me, first." Thea said, pushing her onto the bed and straddling her. She paused as their centers connected. "Mmm."

"Like that, huh?" Rayne teased.

"Very much so," she answered, grinding downward with her swinging hips.

Rayne met the rotations as her hands devoted time to Thea's voluptuous breasts. Thea leaned back, bracing her arms on Rayne's thighs, luxuriating in the sensation of their lovemaking. She felt a hand inch up to her neck, skimming a thumb across kiss-swollen lips. With a wicked smile, Thea locked eyes with Rayne and suckled her thumb. She relinquished control as Rayne pushed and pulled, now with both hands gripping her hips. As soon as Thea's moans picked up volume, Rayne knew she was close. She increased their momentum, causing the bed to scrape against the wall. Thea threw her head back, a thin sheen of perspiration glistened on her skin, the exultation of reaching that pinnacle of release distorting her delicate features. Her body trembled as the dam burst, flowing over Rayne's stomach in waves. Thea slumped into Rayne's arms who immediately rolled until her back hit the comforter.

"Rayne." Thea murmured breathlessly.

"I need to taste you." Rayne kissed her before moving down between her thighs. Wasting no time, she slid her tongue across her hardened nub, grinning at Thea's jerk reaction.

"Play fair, baby."

"I am," Rayne replied before teasing Thea with soft pecks on her labia.

"Mmm. No, you're not."

"I'm savoring the moment."

"Rayne."

Rayne lifted her ass higher and plunged her tongue deep inside Thea's sheath to truly feel her essence. Thea clutched at Rayne's hair, invigorated by the enthusiastic onslaught of her passion. She swiveled her pelvis, following the pirouetting tongue as it dipped and dived through the folds of her femininity. Rayne pushed her legs up, using her tongue to scorch the sensitive walls. Thea bucked against her mouth feeling the climax threatening to burst free. When it arrived, she emitted a low guttural moan and stiffened against the rush of tremors overtaking her body. Rayne didn't acknowledge her climax and continued feasting, pulling Thea closer when she tried to scoot away. Rayne flipped her over again and kissed up the sensitive skin of her back to the nape of her neck before pushing a finger into heated, wet pussy. Thea released another moan, flexing her muscles and squeezing the welcome intruders. She clawed at the comforter, vaguely aware of an arm snaking underneath her body and Rayne's breasts pressed against her. Her moans increased in frequency and volume, all the while Rayne humped, whispering hot, sexy words in her ear.

"I can't get enough of you."

"You can't?" Thea rocked to her rhythm.

"Ever since I first tasted you."

Rayne twisted her fingers to stroke Thea's clit. The resulting explosion caught Thea off guard and a wave of ecstasy coursed through her body. Seconds later, she heard a soft grunt along with the telltale moisture coating her ass. Rayne rolled to the side, giving Thea one more shudder when she removed her fingers. She turned to lay in the crook of Rayne's arms, waiting for their breathing to slow down. Darkness filled every corner of the room, save for the light from the cable box announcing the evening hours. Suddenly, Thea chuckled about the whole situation.

"What's so funny?" Rayne asked, her hand lightly stroking Thea's thigh.

"The interruptions, and your antics."

"My antics?"

"Yes, with Ali."

"Ali needs to buy a reliable car and stop wasting her money," she replied. "And my time."

"She's your friend, baby."

"Who can be a pain in the ass."

Thea sighed. "What am I going to do with you?"

"Well," Rayne smacked her lips. "I do have one more request."

The waterworks returned in response to the smooth, deep tone and she immediately knew the request. Rayne's favorite position. Truth be told, Thea loved it too. "One more request?"

"Yeah, did you forget?" Rayne sharply inhaled when Thea's nails skimmed her breasts.

"How could I?" she replied, lifting her head for a kiss. The hand on her ass became more possessive, pulling her closer to Rayne's nakedness. The fire burned anew, possibly hotter than before. Thea broke the kiss and began the ascent toward the head of the bed with Rayne kissing soft spots of her body along the way. She positioned a knee on either side of Rayne's head and hovered just out of reach. Heavy breathing flitted over her sensitive nub and determined hands cupped her buttocks. Thea held that spot until she felt a warm, wet tongue creep over her labia.

She grasped the quilted headboard for support and began to move back and forth.

"Mmm."

Rayne opened her mouth to spread the length of her tongue from the tip of Thea's pink pearl to the honeypot awaiting attention. Rayne slid her hands up to the small of her back to cradle her body. Thea leaned back, shifting into a slow swirl. Rayne mirrored her movements, alternating between playful nips and feather-like flicks of the tongue. Thea continued to ride, swiveling around as the pressure built and spread throughout her limbs. Rayne pushed inside her again, driving Thea toward yet another summit of rhapsody.

"Fuck." Thea moaned, reaching down to tangle her fingers in Rayne's hair. "Okay, quake."

Rayne felt the vibrations travel up Thea's body and heard the muted moan of her name before a gush of juices coated her cheeks and chin. Thea clung to the headboard, the last bit of energy she had ebbing away. Rayne scooted from under her and watched Thea slide down to the bed. She stretched out next to her wife, wrapping an arm around her waist.

"Happy Valentine's Day." Rayne kissed her cheek.

"Happy Valentine's Day." Thea mumbled with a satisfied sigh. "You could at least wash your face."

"I will in a minute."

"Don't let me fall asleep without washing my ass."

"You're already falling asleep," she said.

"I'm getting up."

"You stay here and nap. I'll run your bath."

"I knew I loved you for a reason," replied Thea, as she wrapped the comforter around her.

Rayne slipped on her robe and decided to add a few points to her account. She returned a short time later to awaken Thea. Candles flickered around the room and the tub, casting dancing shadows on the walls. Rose petals floated in the steaming hot water and filled the darkened room with a pleasing aroma. A frosty glass of Thea's favorite wine waited on the side of the tub.

"You've been busy." Thea settled back on the bath pillow and accepted the offered glass of wine. "Thank you. It's the simple things."

"You're welcome."

"Aren't you joining me?" she asked, with a wicked grin.

"I thought you'd never ask," Rayne admitted.

The next morning, an incoming text message chimed at the usual time, waking Rayne from a peaceful slumber. She rubbed her eyes and glanced over at Thea, snoozing with a serene expression on her beautiful face. Round three began with heavy petting and kissing in the tub and ended with Rayne grinding against Thea on a towel outside the bathroom door. Round four, rumbling stomachs drove them from the bedroom in search of a snack. Soon, Thea expertly kept her balance against the island while Rayne buried her fingers deep in her pussy. After a quick round five in the shower, they finally drifted off, lying in a tangle of arms and legs. Another chirp reminded Rayne of the unread message and she eased from the bed in search of her cell phone. Fresh from the dictionary app, Rayne read the unfamiliar word of the day and in nerdy excitement checked the selection from the day before. She chuckled before abandoning the phone on the nightstand and climbing back in bed. If only she'd read it yesterday.

Anticipation (n): the act of looking forward; especially: a pleasurable expectation

Thank You!

Thank you so much for reading Black Cherry!

If you enjoyed this book, please leave a review, if you're so inclined.

If you ever want to stay in the know about L.M. Bennett's upcoming releases, please be sure to subscribe to the mailing list.